Probability worlds and the eternal search for immortality are the themes of A.E. Van Vogt's brilliant new novel.

What is time? What constitutes the past and the future? Is there a limit to the margins which bind a man?

Or is there no limit to what a man can do once he has the key to the secrets of time?

Let the gifted pen of the author of THE WORLD OF NULL-A and THE WEAPON SHOPS OF ISHER tell you of the Palace of Immortality, of the Possessors, and of the fabulous quest of Peter Caxton for the future.

A.E. VAN VOGT

books available in Ace editions:

THE WAR AGAINST THE RULL

THE WEAPON SHOPS OF ISHER

THE SILKIE

THE UNIVERSE MAKER

THE WEAPON MAKERS

THE FAR-OUT WORLDS OF A.E. VAN VOGT

A.E. VAN VOGT

QUEST FOR THE FUTURE

AN ACE BOOK

Ace Publishing Corporation
1120 Avenue of the Americas
New York, N.Y. 10036

QUEST FOR THE FUTURE

Copyright ©, 1970, by A.E. Van Vogt

All Rights Reserved.

Cover art by John Schoenherr.

Printed in U.S.A.

PROLOGUE

TIME IS THE great unvariant, but the unvariance is no simple relation. Time is here where you are. It is never the same elsewhere. A starbeam penetrates the atmosphere. It brings a picture from seven hundred thousand years in the past. An electron makes a path of light across a cloud chamber. It brings a picture from fifty, a hundred, or more, years in the future. The stars, the world of the finitely large, are always in the past. The world of the immensely, but still finitely, small is always in the future.

This is the rigor of the universe. This is the secret of time.

I

THE HUNDRED DELEGATES to the electronic manufacturers' convention who had attended the showing were drifting toward the doors. Several wives had been present, and their voices mingled with the deeper tones of the men. The sounds faded swiftly into the distance of the hotel, but Señor del Corteya, looking up suddenly from what he was doing, saw that he was still not alone.

He continued rewinding the reel, then put it back into its can and began to pack away the projector. Out of the corner of his eye he watched the other with the curious, speculative intentness of the Latin. At last, his job completed, he turned and said, "Is it me you wish to speak to, señor?"

The big man hesitated, then came forward. He was a tall, chunky, fortyish individual with brown eyes and skimpy hair.

"Odd picture you showed us here tonight."

Corteya smiled his personal acceptance of the compliment. "You were amused, señor?"

Again that hesitation, then, "Where did you get it?"

Corteya shrugged. These direct Americans. Did the man expect him to hand over his trade secrets? He said as much.

"Do you think I am a fool, señor? Perhaps you are planning to start up in opposition to my business. You

7

have plenty of money, maybe, and I go broke when you undercut my prices."

The stranger laughed. But he drew out a card and handed it over. Corteya read:

WALTER DORMAN
President
ELECTRONIC COMPANY OF AMERICA

Corteya looked at it, then handed it back. He saw that Dorman was staring at him hard. The man said finally, with a tiny note of incredulity in his voice, "You still don't believe I'm not after your hide."

Corteya shrugged. "What is it you wish to know, señor?"

"That film?"

Corteya raised his hands in a gesture of deprecation. "A ten-minute novelty."

"Very smoothly done, if you ask me."

"All the world, señor, knows that Hollywood is wonderful."

"Hollywood never made a picture as good as that."

Corteya smiled his if-you-say-so-it-must-be-so smile. Then for the first time he let his mind go back over the picture he had shown. He couldn't remember it very clearly. It was his custom to watch the audience, not the film. Nevertheless, he recollected that it had been about an automatic electric stove that merely had to be supplied with the appropriate ingredients, and it would mix them and serve up the finished meal piping hot at any desired time. He had shown the same film two weeks earlier at a local dieticians' meeting, and the audience had laughed heartily at the nonexistent device.

Corteya said, "Señor, I obtain my films from several

film libraries. Where they secure them, I do not know. They compete for my business. All I do is look over their catalogs and order films when I need them." He lifted his shoulders. "It is as simple as that."

"Have you had any other novelties like the one tonight?"

"A few. I cannot remember."

"Do they all come from the same film library?"

Dorman's persistence was beginning to wear. "I really cannot remember, señor. To me it is all ordinary business."

"Have you any similar films on hand right now?"

"You mean here? No."

"I mean at your office."

Corteya looked unhappy. He was a simple, honest man, who could lie as well as the next, but only if he had started out with a lie, and had to carry on. Having started with the truth, he could not stop.

"At the Aero Club dinner tomorrow," he said gloomily, "I am showing a film about a trip to one of the planets. The catalog says it is very amusing."

Dorman said, "I know this is a lot to ask, but will you drive over to your office, and show me that picture now?"

"Señor, my wife, she is waiting for me at home."

Dorman said nothing. He took out his wallet and peeled off a twenty-dollar bill. As he expected, the other's slim hand reached forth delicately, but without diffidence, and accepted the money.

It took only eight minutes to get to Corteya's place of business, and a few minutes after that the young man's projector was set up and purring.

A seascape broke the shadows of a cloudy but brilliantly bright horizon. The sea was flat, a tideless expanse of water. Suddenly, in those murky depths, there was a stirring. A creature charged into view. It burst the surface and leaped up, twenty, fifty, a hundred feet. Its enormous, bulbous head and vast, yawning mouth seemed almost to touch the camera. And then it began to fall, still struggling, still furiously determined to grasp the prey at which it had leaped.

It failed. It fell. It hit the water with a splash so gigantic that Dorman was startled. He had been admiring the illusion of stark reality that had been produced with what must be an artificial monster-being mechanically activated in some indoor imitation sea. But those splashes looked *real*. A moment later, the narrator said:

"That was a Venusian squid. These creatures, which frequent the depths of the warm seas of Venus, come to the surface only after food. Our camera artist acted as bait, and so enticed the squid to attack him. He was not, however, in danger. Electronic devices protected him at all times."

Dorman smiled twistedly. First an electric stove that prepared meals, now a trip to Venus. Both slick jobs of photography, and, in this case, it was especially clever to suggest there had been no danger. So many of these travelogs about places that actually existed faked suspense and excitement to the point of nausea. He climbed to his feet, his interest close to the vanishing point. He felt very tolerant of himself. Just for a moment, while watching the stove go through its motions, he had had the wild thought that the picture was an advertising stunt for a competitor. The Venusian film put the whole affair into its proper perspective. He saw that Corteya had stopped the machine. The overhead light clicked on.

"Have you learned what you desire?"

"Practically."

The younger man continued to rewind the reel. While he waited, Dorman glanced around the small room. It had a counter at the front. The projector rested on it near the wall. Behind the counter was a single chair and a small set of shelves. That was all the furniture. The whitewashed walls of the office were decorated with still pictures from one-reel and two-reel films. Printed on each of the pictures was a caption giving the subject and the cost of showing. It was obviously a selling business. No one would come into a place like this without having been previously canvassed or told about it in some way.

"What else, señor?"

Dorman turned. The film was in its can, the projector in its case. "I'd like you to check to see if the two films came from the same film library."

"They did, señor." Corteya had not moved. He was smiling in his deprecating fashion. "I looked in the can," he explained, "when I came in."

Dorman made no move to leave. There was nothing else, really, but he hated to leave unfinished anything he had started. Check on everything, then recheck. That was his method, and he had no intention of changing now. He took out his wallet and removed a ten-dollar bill.

"The catalog of this particular library. I'd like to have a look at it."

Corteya accepted the bill and reached under the counter. He came up with several folders. "They send one of these to me every month. These are for the last four months."

Only the final two contained lists of novelty films. Dorman ran his gaze down the column, the smile on his lips broadening. There were several travelogs: Venus, a

11

journey through a Martian desert, a spaceship voyage to the moon, an aerial trip over mountainous Europa, one of the moons of Jupiter, a camera examination of the rings of Saturn, a boat trip down a river of liquid oxygen on Pluto and, finally, the size of the sun as seen from each of its ten planets.

Dorman swiftly glanced at the remaining score or so films given under the novelty heading. He found the one he wanted instantly. The caption was, "Amusing account of an automatic stove that does everything." He closed the folder and paused to look at the address: Arlay Film Library, Lamont Boulevard, in the main part of the city.

"Thanks," said Dorman.

He went out into the street and climbed into his car. It was becoming cooler, so he turned up the windows and sat for a minute lighting a cigarette. Then he drove unhurriedly back to the convention hotel.

II

TEN WEEKS BEFORE, Mr. Lester Arlay, of the Arlay Film Library, had read the first complaint with a faint frown creasing his already lined forehead. The letter had been shoved inside the can of film and it began: "Dear Mr. Arley . . ."

Mr. Arlay started to scowl right there. He did not approve of his name being misspelled. He read on, grimly:

> Dear Mr. Arley:
>   The sound film, "Food Magic," which you sent me is entirely different from what I expected. Neither the audience nor I could make head or tail of it. Certainly, it has nothing to do with food. My program for the retailers' convention here was ruined.

The letter was signed by one of his best customers; and Mr. Arlay, who remembered the two-reeler "Food Magic" perfectly, was dismayed. It was an educational feature turned out by one of the big food distributors. And it was a really dandy job, one of those films which small film libraries could borrow for nothing, and then rent out at a small but profitable rate. It was a film definitely suitable for a grocery retailers' convention.

Frowning, Mr. Arlay shoved the letter back into the can of film and put the can on the "To be Examined" shelf. He began to examine the other ten cans of film that had been returned that morning. Of the ten, four borrowers complained: "This is not the film we asked for." "I cannot understand your sending a film so different from what we ordered." "This is visual gibberish." "Your joke ruined our show."

For several moments, Mr. Arlay stared palely at the letters, and then, with a sudden burst of activity, took one of the films out of its can. He slid the reel onto a projector, made the necessary adjustments, switched off the light, and stared with blank expectancy at the screen.

There was a faraway rustle of music. The music drew closer, but the nearer it came the more uncertainty there was in it. Singing violins played a sweet melody, but a harsher theme quickly intruded, a trill of doubt. The doubt grew and grew until finally the happy strains were completely dominated. Darkly, almost discordantly, the music played—and retreated into distance.

The screen itself came to life. Color flared over it, an intricate weaving movement of color that never quite formed a recognizable pattern. And the rich, vivid colors grew darker and darker until the screen was almost black.

Out of the darkness walked a young woman. She came from the shadows into the light with a casual grace, an agreeable ease, that marked her immediately as one of those marvelous photogenic types. Mr. Arlay had never seen her before, but she quirked her lips into a smile, made a movement with her fingers; and she was a personality.

The trouble was, she had barely appeared when, abruptly, she vanished in a gyrating puff of dark colors. She came on again, and this time she walked along an intense blue hallway into a living room, where a young man sat reading beside a vast window. Mr. Arlay had

14

a flashing glimpse of a city beyond that window; and then the camera angle shifted to the girl.

She was standing behind the man, hesitant. As she stood, the human details of her flesh merged into the dark thematic colors; and it was these colors in human form that moved forward and very obviously kissed the young man on the lips. It was a long kiss, and at the end of it the young man, too, was a color pattern.

The mingled colors began to twist and spin. The screen was a chromatic splendor of gyrating light. It was just beginning to stir with returning music as Mr. Arlay emerged from his puzzlement and held the letter he had received about this particular film in the blazing beam of the projector.

He read: "This is visual gibberish!"

So that was the one! He laid the letter down and held up the can cover with the title on it: "How to Operate a Chicken Farm."

On the screen, the young woman was walking uncertainly along a street, looking back at the man who was coming along slightly behind her. Mr. Arlay clicked it off, rewound the reels, then took another film out of its can. It was the one about which the complainant had said: "Your joke ruined our show."

He threaded the reel into place, and presently a picture of a machine came onto the screen. It was a very bright, clear picture, without any nonsense about it, but the machine was not one that Mr. Lester Arlay could remember having seen before. This fact did not disturb him immediately. The world was full of machines that he had never seen and, what was more, never wanted to see. He waited, and a quiet baritone said: "No spaceman should have any difficulty repairing this new space drive."

Mr. Arlay sighed, and lifted the can cover to the light. The title on it was: "How to Operate the American Cogshill Diesel Engine."

What had happened was clear enough, it seemed to Mr. Arlay. Somebody had returned a whole series of wrong films to him, and he had sent them out in their original cans. The fantastic bad-luck angle of the affair was that no less than five wrong films had gone out all at once.

On the screen, the baritone voice was saying, "Now, raise the drive case itself. Since the standard weight of the case is eight tons, care must be taken when near a planetary body to balance the antigravity needles at a similitude of ninety-nine gravitons. Unwringing them becomes a matter of one good shove—"

Mr. Arlay shut the film off, and he was packing it into a can when the thought came: *What did he say?* What *did he say?*

He stood owlishly blinking his realization that something was very wrong.

There was an interruption. The outer door opened, and a young woman came in. She wore a mink coat, and heavily jeweled rings flashed on her fingers. " 'Lo, honey," she said in a husky voice.

Mr. Arlay, all extraneous thoughts flying from his mind, came around the counter. His wife skillfully evaded the kiss he attempted to plant on her lips.

"Have you any money?" she asked. "I'm going shopping."

Mr. Arlay said, "Careful, Tania. We're almost at rock bottom."

He said it affectionately. He tried to kiss her again, and this time managed to brush her cheek. His words made her shake her slim body impatiently.

"That's all I ever hear from you," she said darkly. "Why don't you make money like some of the people in this town?"

Mr. Arlay almost pointed out that he did. He refrained. He had no illusions about his hold on this young woman. His business netted him between three and five hundred dollars a week. It was not a terrific amount of money, but it rivaled the salaries of many featured movie players. They might make a little more per week, but few of them made it fifty-two weeks a year. It was that income which had enabled him, on one of his visits to Hollywood three years before, to marry a small-part player who was a far more attractive person physically than he could have hoped to marry without money. Mentally—that was another matter. She was a survival type in a sense that would have startled Darwin. Regardless of the variation in his income, she managed to spend it all, month in, month out. Her adaptability sometimes amazed even that defeatist, Mr. Arlay.

He did not realize, however, the profound influence she had had on him. All the imaginative qualities that had built his business had been replaced by a complete dependence on experience. He regarded himself as a practical man, and he had no inkling that his habit of thinking of himself as "Mr." was but one compensation for the psychic disaster he had suffered when she entered his life.

Not that he would necessarily have suspected that he had come into possession of films that had been made a hundred or more years in the future.

Now that she had come into the office, he strove to keep her there. "Got something here that might interest you," he said eagerly. "Somebody sent me a film of

17

some other library by mistake, and it's quite an odd affair, a sort of visual freak."

"Now, darling, I'm in a hurry, and—"

Her narrowed eyes saw that this was no moment to refuse him. He needed an occasional crumb, and he was so *completely* unsuspicious. After all, she'd be a nut to let this soft touch walk out on her.

"All right, honey," she crooned. "If you want me to."

He showed her the film with the man and the girl and the swirling colors—and realized the moment the girl appeared on the screen that he had made a mistake. His wife stiffened as that superb actress came into view.

"Hmm," she said bitingly. "What kind of ham are you serving up now?"

Mr. Arlay let the film run its course without another word. He had momentarily forgotten that his wife did not admire other actresses, particularly stars. Watching the film, he absently noticed that the reason for the dark tones of music and color seemed to be that the girl was unhappily married, and the twisting colors were designed to show her changing emotions, the doubts that came, and the thoughts that welled up in her mind.

Interesting, he thought. *I wonder who made it.*

As the reel ended, Tania jumped to her feet. "Well, got to be running. I'll cash a check for five hundred dollars. Okay?"

"Three!" said Mr. Arlay.

"Four," said his wife in a tone of friendly give and take.

Four hundred it was. When she was gone, Mr. Arlay began a checkup to see who had sent him the unusual films. The card index for the film, "How to Operate a Chicken Farm," gave a list of men and schools and institutions that had rented the item. The second to last rentor would obviously be the one. His gaze flashed down to it.

"Tichenor Collegiate," he read.

Mr. Arlay frowned at the name, and mentally changed the wording of the letter he intended to write. Tichenor Collegiate was easily one of his best customers. And, what was more, the operator in charge, Peter Caxton, a science teacher, was a thoroughly experienced man. It scarcely seemed possible that Caxton could be guilty.

Mr. Arlay quickly examined the card for another of the eccentric films. The second to last borrower was Tichenor Collegiate. The same name came up for each of the three others returned to him, and which didn't belong to his library. Mr. Arlay sat down at his typewriter and, bearing in mind that customers were seldom offended by the facts of the case, wrote:

Dear Mr. Caxton:

A number of films which you have returned to us were not the ones which we originally sent you. Altogether five films

He paused there. Five? How did he know there were only five? Mr. Arlay made a beeline for the Tichenor Collegiate's personal file card. It was a thick one, additions having been glued to it from time to time.

He skipped down to the fifteenth name on the card. That would take it back just a little over two weeks. The title was: "Pruning Fruit Trees." The film itself, when Mr. Arlay viewed it, was a fantastic concoction in which a curiously shaped ship seemed to leave the Earth's surface and go to the Moon. The illusions were very realistic, and the photography had a Hollywood slickness.

Mr. Arlay shut it off finally, thinking for the first time that whoever was making those pictures would be well worth representing.

Meanwhile, there was a job to do. One by one, he screened the last nineteen films that had been borrowed by Tichenor. That is, he screened the sixteen that were in. Three had been re-rented and, in due course, no doubt, he would hear from them.

Of the sixteen, seven were travelogs. Travelogs—unique, incredible creations, filmed by a madman. But mad or not, he was a genius, and he had designed some of the most lifelike backgrounds ever conceived for fantasia. Among the first few that Mr. Arlay screened was the one about Venus which, ten weeks later, Pedro del Corteya showed to electronics manufacturer Walter Dorman. Mr. Arlay watched it and the other reels about the solar system with an appraising eye. There was, it seemed to him, much to be said for a skillful motion-picture presentation of what science believed about the various planetary bodies.

Seven travelogs and eight how-to-operate or how-to repair films—one dealing with the operation of a meaningless engine. At least it seemed meaningless to Mr. Arlay. It had a single extrusion in a strong boxing. There were little chambers in the boxing, and when they were filled with a fine metallic powder, the extrusion could be made to turn with a velocity that did not slow when it was connected with a large machine of intricate construction. Another film dealt with the repair of what was called an atomic gun. Here, too, the fine metallic powder was tamped into tiny chambers, but there was a transformation tunnel, the purpose of which was not clear. When fired, the gun, a hand weapon, blew a four-hundred-foot-high hill into dust.

Mr. Arlay became impatient as the eight films unreeled onto the screen. This was going a little too far. The travelogs had a certain scientific value, but these operation and repair films, with their pretense to detail, strained all credulity. An atomic engine and an atomic gun. How to repair a space drive. Care and operation of the Fly-O, an individual flyer—a combination of straps and a metallic tube that lifted the man in the film off the ground and transported him through the air like Buck Rogers. A radio that was simply a bracelet made of what was called "sensitive metal." The crystalline structure of the sensitivity was detailed, and the radio waves were shown transformed into sound by ultra-thin bubbles in the metal. There were three rather amusing films about household devices. There was a light which focused wherever desired out of thin air; rugs and furniture that couldn't get dirty; and finally, the automatic stove that was later to rouse Walter Dorman's competitive instincts. Long before the showing was finished, it had struck Mr. Arlay that there was a type of audience that would be interested in such novelties. It would be important, however, to stress the novelty angle, so that the people would be prepared to laugh.

His best bet, of course, would be to locate their source, and stock a few himself. He phoned Tichenor Collegiate, and asked for Caxton. Caxton said:

"My dear Mr. Arlay, it cannot possibly be we who are at fault. To prevent confusion in bookkeeping, I have long adopted a policy of renting from only one library at a time. For the past two months we have secured our material from you, and returned it promptly. Perhaps you had better reexamine your files."

His tone was faintly patronizing, and there was just enough suggestion of an affronted customer in it to make Mr. Arlay back down.

"Yes, yes, of course. I'll have a look at them myself. My helper must have ... uh ..."

Mr. Arlay hung up, saw that it was nearly one o'clock, and went out to lunch. He drove all the way up to Main Street for a bowl of tomato soup. The fever in him died slowly, and he realized that it was actually not a difficult situation. He had lost nineteen films, but if he wrote careful letters to the firms that had supplied them to him they would probably send him new ones immediately. And as a sort of compensation for the wear and tear on his nerves, he had sixteen, possibly nineteen, novelty films which might go over rather well.

They did. At least once a week the novelties went out into the mails, and returned again. And by the time they came back there were orders waiting for most of them for the following week. Mr. Arlay did not worry about what the real owner of the films would think when he discovered what was happening. No single library film was worth very much. The owner would probably demand the wholesaler's percentage, and this Mr. Arlay was prepared to pay.

And just in case audience reaction would be required, Mr. Arlay sent printed forms for comments. They came back properly filled out. The size of the audience: one hundred, two hundred, seventy-five. The nature of the audience: retailers' dinner, university astronomy class, the society of physicists, high school students. The reaction of the audience—comments most often made: amusing, interesting, good photography. One common criticism was that the dialog could be more humorous, befitting the nature of the subject matter.

The situation did not remain static. At the end of the second month, Mr. Arlay had thirty-one more novelty films, and every one of them had been sent to him by Peter Caxton of Tichenor Collegiate.

After ten weeks, just about the time that Pedro del Corteya was due to show the stove picture to the electronic manufacturers' convention, two things happened approximately simultaneously: Mr. Arlay raised the rent of the novelties fifty percent, and Caxton sent him a letter, which read in part: "I have noticed in your folders a reference to some novelty films. I would like one dealing with a planet for next Wednesday."

Now, thought Mr. Arlay, *now we shall see.*

The can came back on Thursday. The film inside was also a novelty type. But it was not the same one he had sent out.

III

On his way to Tichenor Collegiate for the afternoon classes, Peter Caxton stopped in the corner drugstore and bought a pack of cigarettes. There was a full-length mirror just in front of the door. As he emerged, he paused briefly to survey himself in it.

The picture he saw pleased him. His tall form was well dressed, his face clean but not too youthful, and his eyes were a smiling gray. The well-groomed effect was accentuated by a neat gray hat. He walked on, content. Caxton had no illusions about life. Life was what you made it. And as far as he could see, if he worked things right, he ought to be principal of Tichenor in another two years. The time limit was unavoidable. Old Varnish was not due for retirement until then, and Caxton could see no way by which the process could be speeded up.

Tichenor was no super-school, nor did it have the fancy money behind it that some neighboring communities raised every year for education. The smoking room for the men and women was a joint affair. Caxton settled into one of the chairs and puffed quickly at his cigarette. He was about halfway through when Miss Gregg came in.

She smiled warmly. " 'Lo, Peter," she said. Her gaze flashed significantly to the closed doors of the men's and women's dressing rooms, then back to him.

Caxton said, "Nobody in the men's."

She opened the door to the women's, glanced in, then came over in a gliding motion and planted a kiss on his lips.

"Careful," said Peter Caxton.

"Tonight," she said in a low tone, "at the end of the park."

Caxton could not suppress a faint look of irritation. "I'll try," he said, "but my wife—"

She whispered fondly, "I'll expect you."

The door closed softly behind her. Caxton sat frowning, disturbed. At first it had been pleasant, his conquest of Miss Gregg's heart. But after six months of ever more frequent rendezvous, the affair was beginning to be a little wearing. She had reached the stage where she anticipated that somehow he would manage to get a divorce, and that somehow it would not hurt his career, and that somehow everything would come out all right. Caxton shared neither her anxiety for such a culmination nor her vague conviction that there would be no repercussions.

Miss Gregg, he realized too late, was an emotional fool. For a month he had known that he must break off with her, but so far only one method had occurred to him: she must be eased out of the school. How? The answer to that, too, had come easily. A whispering campaign against her and Dorrit. That way he could kill two birds with one stone. Dorrit was his only serious rival for the principalship and, what was worse, he and Old Varnish got along very well.

It shouldn't be very hard. Everybody except Miss Gregg knew that Dorrit was nuts about her, and Dorrit didn't seem to suspect that his secret was known. The situation amused Caxton. He, a married man, had walked off with Dorrit's dream girl. There was no reason why he shouldn't also snatch the principalship from under Dorrit's nose, so to speak. He'd have to think a little more about the moves, and proceed with the utmost caution.

Caxton rubbed his cigarette into an ash tray with a speculative thoughtfulness, then he headed for the auditorium. His first class was to have a film showing—a nuisance, those things. In the beginning, he had been quite interested, but there were too many poor films. Besides, the dopes never learned anything anyway. He had once questioned some of the brighter students about what they had learned from a film, and it was pitiful. Proponents, however, maintained that the effect was cumulative, the kids preferred it to other methods of teaching, and last week the school board had ordered that Grade Ten, as well as Grade Eleven, was to be shown each film.

That meant that once in the morning, once in the afternoon, he had to handle a swarm of teenagers in the darkness of an auditorium. At least this was the last showing for today. The film had been running for about a minute when Caxton took his first real look at the screen. He stared for a moment blankly, then shut off the projector, turned on the lights, and came down from the projection room.

"Who's responsible for this silly trick?" he asked angrily.

No one answered. The girls looked a little scared, the boys stiffened, except for a few teachers' pets, who turned pale.

"Somebody," Caxton shouted, "has switched films on me over the lunch hour."

He stopped. His own words jarred him. He had

26

charged out of the projection booth without pausing to assess the implications of what had happened. Now, suddenly, he realized. For the first time in his four years at Tichenor he had been the victim of a student's prank, and he was taking it badly. After a moment of further thought, he made an even greater mental adjustment, and the situation was saved.

Caxton swallowed hard. A wan smile lighted his tense face. He looked around coolly. "Well," he said, "if this is what you want, you'll get it."

The second day his smile was grimmer, and it became a matter of discipline. "If this," he said, "happens again, I shall have to report to Old Varn—" He stopped. He had been about to say "Old Varnish." He finished instead, properly—"report to Mr. Varney."

It was a shaken and somewhat mystified Caxton who went into the principal's office the following day. "But where do they obtain the replacement films?" the old man asked helplessly. "After all, they cost money."

The question was not his final word. On Thursday, the film again being different, he trotted dutifully to each of the two classes, and pointed out the unfairness of their action. He also indicated that, since the lost films would have to be paid for, the affair was beginning to take on a decidedly criminal aspect.

The fifth day was Friday, and it was evident that the students had talked things over, for the president of each of the two classes made a brief denial of the suspicions of the faculty. "As you probably know," said one, "the students are usually aware of what is going on among themselves. But this class as a whole is unaware of the identity of the guilty party. Whoever is changing the films is playing a lone hand, and we herewith denounce him, and withdraw any support or sympathy we might normally give to such a student."

The words should have quieted Caxton's nerves. But they had the reverse effect. His first conviction, that he was being made game of by the students, had already partly yielded to a wilder thought, and the speeches merely enlivened the newer feeling. That afternoon at recess, without proper forethought, he made the mistake of voicing the suspicion to the principal.

"If the students are not to blame, then one of the teachers must be. And the only one I know who dislikes me intensely is Dorrit." He added grimly, "If I were you, I would also investigate the relationship between Miss Gregg and Dorrit."

Varney showed a surprising amount of initiative. The truth was, the old man was easily tired, and he was already worn out by the affair. He called both Miss Gregg and Dorrit, and, to Caxton's dismay, repeated the accusations, Miss Gregg flashed one amazed look at the stunned Caxton, and then sat rigid throughout the rest of the meeting. Dorrit looked angry for a moment, then he laughed.

"This week," he said, "has been an eye-opener for most of us here. We have seen Caxton wilt under the conviction that the student body didn't like him. I always thought he was a highly developed neurotic, and now in five days he has shown that he is worse than anything I imagined. Like all true neurotics of the more advanced kind, he failed to make even the most elementary investigations before launching his accusations. For instance, his first charge. I can disprove that since, for at least two days this week, I could not possibly have been near the projection room."

He proceeded to do so. He had been sick at his boarding house on Tuesday and Wednesday.

"As for the second and more unforgivable accusation, I only wish it were true, though in a different sense than Caxton has implied. I am one of those shy individuals where women are concerned, but under the circumstances I can say that I have long been a distant admirer of Miss Gregg."

The young woman showed her first vague interest at that point. From the corner of her eye she glanced at Dorrit, as if she were seeing him in a new light. The glance lasted only a moment, then she returned to her tensed contemplation of the wall straight in front of her. Dorrit was continuing:

"It is difficult, of course, to disprove anything as vague as the charge Mr. Caxton has leveled, but—"

Old Varnish cut him off. "It is quite unnecessary to say anything further. I do not for one moment believe a word of it, and I cannot understand what Mr. Caxton's purpose could have been, to introduce such an ill-considered accusation into this wretched affair of the lost films. If the film situation does not rectify, I shall report to the school board at their meeting next week, and we shall have an investigation. That is all. Good day, gentlemen. Good day, Miss Gregg."

Caxton spent a confused weekend. He was pretty sure that the principal had derived satisfaction from the situation, but there was nothing to do about that except curse himself for having provided the man with the opportunity to get rid of an unwanted heir to his own position. The worst confusion, however, had nothing to do with Varney. Caxton had the sinking feeling that things were happening behind his back. The feeling turned out to be correct.

On Monday morning all the women teachers snubbed him, and most of the men were distinctly unfriendly. One of the men walked over and said in a low tone, "How did you happen to make such a charge against Gregg and Dorrit?"

"I was beside myself with worry," Caxton said miserably. "I was not in my right senses."

"You sure weren't," said the other. "Gregg's told all the women."

Caxton thought grimly, *A woman scorned.*

The other man finished, "I'll try to do what I can but . . ."

It was too late. At lunchtime the women teachers entered the principal's office in a body, and announced that they would refuse to work in the same school with a male teacher capable of such an untrue story about one of them. Caxton, who had already permitted himself flashing thoughts on the possibility of resignation, was now confronted by the necessity of an actual decision. He resigned at intermission, the separation to take effect at the end of the month, the following weekend.

His action cleared the air. The male teachers were friendlier, and his own mind slowly and painfully straightened out. By Tuesday he was thinking savagely but with clarity: *Those films! If it hadn't been for that mixup, I wouldn't have lost my head. If I could find out who was responsible . . .*

It seemed to him that the resulting satisfaction would almost compensate him for the loss of his job. He did not go home for lunch. He only pretended to start out. Swiftly, he doubled back to the rear entrance and, hurrying to the projection room, concealed himself behind a substitute screen that stood against the wall.

He waited during the entire lunch period. Nothing happened. Nobody tampered with the locked doors of the auditorium. No one came near the door of the projection room. And after lunch, when he started the projector, the film was different.

In the morning it had been an ordinary film, concerned with daily farming. The afternoon film was about the development and use of chemicals to thin or thicken the human blood, and so enable human beings to fit themselves overnight for extreme changes in temperature.

It was the first time that Caxton had closely examined one of the strange novelty films, of which he had ordered several about two weeks before. Examined it, that is, with his mind as well as his eyes, and was amazed. *Who is making those pictures?* he thought. *Why they're wonderful, so full of ideas that . . .*

He returned to the projection room after school for another look. And received the shock of his life. It was a different film. Different from the one in the morning. Different from the one after lunch. It was a third film, its subject the inside of the sun. With trembling fingers, Caxton rewound the film, and ran it through again. The perspiration came out on his face as an entirely different, fourth film, unwound on the screen. The wild impulse came to rush down to the office to phone Varney. That ended with the realization that the man would refuse. The principal had implied at least twice that the film tangle would probably rectify the moment Caxton left. The burden of weariness that he wore made him cling to that conviction. "Tomorrow," he would say. "I'll have a look at the projector tomorrow."

It couldn't wait until tomorrow, or so it seemed to Caxton. For the first time, he remembered the phone call he had received more than two months before from Mr. Arlay of the Arlay Film Library. The memory cooled him off. His second impulse within minutes—this time to call Arlay—faded before a recollection of what he had said to that man. He had been, he remembered, rather snooty. He'd phone Arlay later.

He sat down and puffed at a cigarette, thinking nervously: *Here is the most remarkable instrument in the twentieth century.* And thinking of how he could get hold of it and keep it for himself.

His final answer to that question grew out of an observation he had made at an early age, when he had first noticed that what his mother didn't see him do she didn't complain about.

He went down into the basement of the school and secured a piece of sacking. Next, he removed the projector from its mounting and wrapped it securely. And carried it to his car. Returning, he grabbed all the films that he knew had been through the projector, and took them along in a paper bag.

Let them figure out what had happened. The disappearance of the projector would seem like some sort of final mystery at the end of a week of confusion.

And, of course, he would deny all knowledge.

As a special precaution he drove all the way into the city, and rented storage space for the machine, using an assumed name.

It was nearly seven o'clock when he arrived home for dinner, and, naturally, Lucy was mad. But Caxton had already analyzed that the whole story of the school affair would shortly come out, and he was in process of hardening himself against the poisonous atmosphere that, he predicted to himself, a little shaken at the prospect, would result. Yet he also anticipated that the consequent nightmare would provide him with an opportunity to divorce a woman who had aged faster than he.

Incredibly, his wife filed suit for divorce against him. . . . It seemed incredible to Caxton, because he had expected that she would try to hold onto him, and that he would have to fight his way out of the marriage.

He was free to pursue his fantastic search.

Caxton saw his first step as finding the Quik-Photo Supply Corporation, from which firm he himself had ordered the motion picture projector for the school a few months earlier. A used machine, shrewdly purchased by him at a low price as one of many actions that would show that he would make a frugal school principal, it undoubtedly had a history.

That had to be the trail.

IV

THE HOSPITAL bed was hard under his body. For a moment it seemed to Caxton that this was what was bothering him. He turned over into a more comfortable position, and knew it wasn't physical at all. It was something in his mind, the sense of emptiness that had been there since they had told him the date.

After what seemed a long time, the door opened, and two men and a nurse came in. One of the men said in a hearty voice, "Well, how are you Caxton? It's a shame to see you down like this."

The man was plumpish, a good-fellow type. Caxton accepted his vigorous handshake, lay very still for a moment, and then allowed the awkward but very necessary question to escape his lips. "I'm sorry," he said stiffly, "but do I know you?"

The man said, "I'm Bryson, sales manager of the Quik-Photo Supply Corporation. Two weeks ago, I hired you and put you on the road as a salesman. The next thing I knew, you were found unconscious in a ditch, and the hospital advised me you were here." He finished, "You had identification papers on you connecting you with us."

Caxton nodded. But he was disappointed. He had thought it would be enough to have someone fill a gap in his mind. It wasn't. He said finally, "My last remembrance is my decision to apply for a job with your firm.

34

Apparently something happened to my mind at that point, and—"

He stopped. His eyes widened at the thought that this might be connected with his search for the origin of the motion picture projector. He said slowly, conscious of an unpleasant sensation, "Apparently, I've had amnesia."

He saw that the house doctor, who had come in with Bryson, was looking at him sharply. Caxton mustered a wan smile. "I guess it's all right, Doc. What gets me is the kind of life I must have lived these last two weeks. I've been lying here straining my brain. There's something in the back of my mind, but I can't remember what."

The doctor was smiling behind his pince-nez. "I'm glad you're taking it so well. Nothing to worry about, really. As for what you did, I assure you that our experience has been that the victim of amnesia usually lives a reasonably normal life. One of the most frequent characteristics is that the victim takes up a different occupation. You didn't even do that."

He paused, and the plump Bryson chimed in heartily, "I can clear up the first week for you. You spent a couple of days looking over our stock and checking our sources of supply. And then you told me that you had lived for a while as a boy in some village on the Warwick Junction-Kissling line. And that you would like to have that as your first route. I gave it to you."

It was his first piece of real information—and Caxton restrained himself with difficulty. Since he had never lived in any such place, *that* must be the area to which he had traced the projector. . . . He grew aware that Bryson was still speaking:

"We had orders from you from five towns on the way,

but you never got to Kissling. Maybe that will help you. . . . No?" The man shrugged. "Well, never mind. As soon as you're up, Caxton, come and see me. In these days of ever more complicated electronic equipment, I'm glad to have an M.A. in physics on the staff. In fact, I'm dickering with some new representations, with you in mind as the man to handle them. There'll be lots more money potential, so get well quickly."

Caxton said, "Right now, I'd like to have the same territory, if it's all right."

Bryson nodded. "Mind you, it's only a matter of finishing up what you missed before, and then moving further along the main line. Those other representations will take a while to organize. So the Kissling route is yours. I guess you want to check up on what happened to you."

"That," said Caxton, "is exactly what I have in mind. A sort of search for my memory."

He managed a grim smile as he thought, *I must have found something* . . . and that was the *real* search.

Fear touched him. He fought it down, said, "I want to thank you for coming."

"That's all right. So long."

Bryson shook hands warmly, and Caxton watched him out of the door.

V

TWO DAYS LATER, Caxton climbed off the Transcontinental at Warwick Junction, and stood blinking in the bright sun of early morning. His first disappointment had already come. He had hoped that the sight of the cluster of houses silhouetted against the line of hills would bring his memory back.

Too obviously, his mind was not being jarred into the faintest remembrance of what he had done or seen sixteen days earlier. Caxton shook his head in bewilderment. *Somebody knew me*, he thought. *Somebody must have seen me. I talked to storekeepers, travelers, trainmen, hotel men. I've always been able to pretend that I'm a sociable type. . . .*

"Hello, there, Caxton, old chap," said a cheerful voice beside him. "You look as if you're thinking about a funeral."

Caxton turned and saw a rather slender young man, dark-faced and dark-haired, about thirty years old. He had the slouch of a too-thin person who had carried too many sample cases. He must have noticed something in Caxton's eyes, for he said quickly, "You do remember me, don't you? Bill Kellie." He laughed easily. "Say, come to think of it, I've got a bone to pick with you. What did you do with that girl, Selanie? I've been past Piffer's Road twice since I saw you last, and she didn't come around either time. She—" He stopped and his gaze was suddenly sharp. "Say, you do remember me, don't you?"

Caxton emerged from his intense inner excitement, and realized from the expression on Kellie's face that it was time to explain. He did so, finishing finally, "So you see, I'm in quite a mental fix. Maybe, if you don't mind, you could give me some idea of what happened while I was with you. Who is this girl, Selanie?"

"Oh, sure," said Kellie, "sure I'll . . ." He paused, frowned. "You're not kidding me, are you?" He waved Caxton silent. "Okay, okay, I'll believe you. We've got half an hour before the Kissling local is due. Amnesia, eh? I've heard about that stuff, but—say, you don't think that old man could have anything to do with—" He banged his right fist into his left palm. "I'll bet that's it."

"An old man!" Caxton said. He caught himself, finished firmly, "What about this story?"

The train slowed. Through the streaky window Caxton could see a rolling valley with patches of green trees and a gleaming, winding thread of water. Then some houses came into view, half a dozen siding tracks, and finally the beginning of a wooden platform.

A tall, slim, fine-looking girl walked past his window carrying a basket. Behind Caxton, the traveling salesman who had come aboard at the last stop and to whom he had been talking said, "Oh, there's Selanie. I wonder what kind of super-gadget she's got for sale today."

Caxton leaned back in his seat, and his mind slowly fastened on what the other had said. "Selanie!" he echoed then. "Curious name. Did you say she sells things?"

"*Does* she sell things!" Kellie spoke explosively.

He must have realized the forcefulness of his words, for he drew a deep, audible breath. His blue eyes looked hard into Caxton's. He started to say something, stopped himself, and finally sat smiling a secret smile. After a moment, he said, "You know, I really must apologize. I've just now realized that I've monopolized the conversation ever since we started talking."

Caxton smiled with polite tolerance. "You've been very entertaining."

Kellie persisted. "What I mean by that is, it's just penetrated to me that you told me you sold photo supplies, among other things."

Caxton shrugged. He wondered if he looked as puzzled as he was beginning to feel. He watched as Kellie drew out a picture print and held it out for him to take. Kellie said, "See anything odd about that?"

Caxton's first glance saw it as a masterful color print. He had a hard time focusing on it because in the back of his mind he was waiting for one of those pointless arguments about the relative merits of the supplies he was selling. In the first place he didn't give a damn, and in the second place—well, to hell with it!

As he had these thoughts, he was trying to look at the print. It was almost as if he suddenly saw the scene for what it was then. And realized with a mental leap of excitement that he had seen it before: The same Venusian ocean scene as in one of the novelty films that he had secured from the Arlay Film Library while he was with Tichenor Collegiate. At least, it looked the same.

Caxton's fingers tightened on the print. "Hey," he said, "where did you get this?"

"From Selanie," was the triumphant reply.

Caxton studied the beautiful, wild, watery scene with its crazy monster more closely—and more relaxedly. It was fortunate, he told himself, that it *was* the Venusian scene. Sort of put the whole thing into a more ordinary perspective, because of course the Venus probes of the Great Powers had by now thoroughly established that Venus was not a steaming replica of the warm seas of prehistoric Earth. Instead, it was a super-hot desert with surface temperatures ranging high enough to melt many metals.

He started to hand the print back to the younger man. "Pretty good," he said. "Somebody's pretty slick at art-work. I'd like to meet this girl, Selanie."

"Hold on," said Kellie. "There's more."

He reached over and touched the print, squeezing one edge slightly. "Now look," he said.

Caxton glanced down casually. For a moment—for just a moment—he was calm and merely expectant. And then there was an instant of mental blur and, finally, a gloppy confusion inside him as if all his innards had jumped simultaneously in different directions.

As from a distance, he heard Kellie say, "I told you there was something odd about the print."

"Odd!" It took a few seconds for Caxton to realize that the croaking voice had been his own.

The next instant he was just staring.

The scene on, or *in*, the print . . . moved. The waves churned. The creature with the huge lizard head, so reminiscent of the beasts that roamed the watery swamps of forty million years before on Earth, was going through its act of trying to capture the man who was hovering above the waves. It came rushing forward. Its mouth gaped. It launched itself from the water. Tantalizingly, the man rose up on his Fly-O, staying out of reach of the razor teeth that pushed so savagely up toward him.

The attack sequence ran its course as Caxton watched. The picture came to a stop exactly when the gigantic jaws filled the entire print. At that point there was a peculiar blurring effect and then . . . the jaws faded. The scene was back again to what it had been when Caxton first took the print from Kellie's hand.

Unmoving, silent, beautiful, crazy.

Presumably, ready to wind through its little sequence again.

Caxton held the remarkable thing like a connoisseur caressing a priceless jewel. As from a great distance he heard Kellie chattering on. "Her father makes them," he was saying. "He's a genius with gadgets. You ought to see some of the stuff she's been selling on this train the last month. One of these days he's going to get wise to himself and start large-scale manufacture. When that day comes, all photography companies and a lot of other firms go out of business."

It was a thought that had already occurred to Caxton. Before he could muster his mind for speech, the print was taken from his fingers, and Kellie was leaning across the aisle toward a handsome gray-haired man. Kellie said, "I noticed you looking at this, sir, while I was showing it to my friend. Would you like to examine it?"

"Why, yes," said the man.

He spoke in a low tone, but the sound had a resonance that tingled in Caxton's ears. The old man's fingers grasped the extended print and, just like that, the print broke into several pieces.

"Oh!" Kellie exclaimed blankly.

"I beg your pardon," said the fine looking old man. A dollar bill appeared in his hand. "That was my fault, I'm afraid. But you can buy another one from the girl when she comes." He leaned back in his seat, and buried himself behind a newspaper.

Caxton saw that Kellie was biting his lip. The young

man sat staring at the pieces of his broken print, then at the dollar bill, and then in the direction of the now hidden face of the gray-haired man. At last Kellie sighed. "I can't understand it. I've had the print a month. It has twice fallen into water, and has been exposed to heat without damage—and now it crumbles like a piece of rotted wood." He shrugged, but his tone was complaining as he went on after a moment, "I suppose you can't really expect Selanie's father to do a first-rate job with the facilities he's—" He broke off excitedly. "Oh, look, there's Selanie now. I wonder what she's featuring today." A sly smile crept into his narrow face. "Just wait until I confront her with that ruined print. I kidded her when I bought it, told her there must be a trick to it. She got mad then, and guaranteed it for life. What the devil is she selling anyway? Look, they're crowding around her."

Caxton climbed to his feet. He craned his neck the better to see over the heads of the crowd that was watching the girl demonstrate something at the far end of the car.

"Good heavens!" a man's deep voice exclaimed. "How much are you charging for those cups? How do they work?"

"Cups!" said Caxton, and moved toward the group in a haze of fascination. If he had seen right, the girl was handing around a container which kept filling full of liquid. And people would drink, and it would fill up again instantly. Somehow, Caxton thought, her father had learned to precipitate liquids. There was genius here. And if he could make a deal with the man for himself, he was made.

The tremendous thought ended, as the girl's crystal-clear voice rose above the excited babble. "The price is one dollar each. It works by chemical condensation of gases in the air. The process is known only to my father. But wait, I haven't finished my demonstration."

She went on, her voice cool and strong in the silence that settled around her. "As you see, it's a folding drinking cup without a handle. First, you open it. Then you turn the top strip clockwise. At a certain point, water comes. But now—watch. I'm turning it further. The liquid turns red and becomes a sweet-sourish drink that is very refreshing in hot weather."

She handed the cup around. While it was being passed from fingers to clutching fingers, Caxton managed to wrench his gaze from the gadget and really look at the girl. She was tall, about five feet six, and she had dark brown hair. Her face was unmistakably of a fine intelligence. It was thin and good-looking, and there was an odd proud tilt to it that gave her a startling appearance of aloofness in spite of the way she was taking the dollar bills that were being thrust at her.

Once again, her voice rose, "I'm sorry, only one to a person. They'll be on the general market one of these days. These are only souvenirs."

The crowd dissolved, each person returning to his or her seat. The girl came along the aisle, and stopped in front of Caxton. Caxton said quickly, "My friend here showed me a photoprint you were selling. I wonder—"

"I still have a few." She nodded gravely. "Would you like a cup, also?"

Caxton nodded toward Kellie. "My friend here would like another print, too. His tore."

"I'm sorry, I can't sell him a second print." She paused. Her eyes widened. She said with a weighty slowness, "Did you say his *tore?*"

Astoundingly, she swayed. She said wildly, "Let me see that? Where is it?"

She took the pieces of the photoprint from Kellie's fingers and stared at them. Her mouth began to tremble. Her hands shook. Her face took on a gray, drawn look. Her voice, when she spoke, was a whisper. "Tell me . . . how did it happen? *Exactly* how?"

"Why"—Kellie drew back in surprise—"I was handing it to that old gentleman over there when—"

He stopped, because he had lost his audience. The girl spun on her heel. It was like a signal. The old man lowered his paper and looked at her. She stared back at him with the fascinated expression of a bird cornered by a snake. Then, for the second time within two minutes, she swayed. The basket nearly dropped from her hand as she ran, but somehow she hung on to it as she careened along the aisle.

A moment later, Caxton saw her racing across the platform. She became a distant, running form on Piffer's Road.

"What the hell!" Kellie exploded.

He whirled on the old man. "What did you do to her?" he demanded fiercely. "You—"

His voice sank into silence, and Caxton, who had been about to add his hard words to the demand, remained quiet also.

VI

THE SALESMAN'S voice there under the bright sun on the platform at Warwick Junction faded. It required a moment for Caxton to grasp that the story had ended.

"You mean that's all?" he demanded. "We just sat there like a couple of dummies, out-faced by an old man? And that was the end of the business? You still don't know what scared the girl?"

He saw on Kellie's face the strange look of a man who was searching mentally for a word or phrase to describe the indescribable. Kellie said finally:

"There was something about him like . . . like all the tough sales managers in the world rolled into one, and feeling their orneriest. We just shut up."

Caxton nodded grimly, said slowly, "He didn't get off?"

"No, you were the only one who got off."

"Eh?"

Kellie looked at him. "You know, this is the damnedest, funniest thing. But that's the way it was. You asked the trainman to check your bags at Inchney. The last thing I saw of you before the train pulled out, you were walking up Piffer's Road in the direction the girl had gone and— Ah, here comes the Kissling local now."

The combination freight and passenger train edged in noisily. . . . Later, as it was winding in and out along the edge of a valley, Caxton sat staring at the terrain, only vaguely conscious of Kellie's chattering beside him.

45

He decided finally on the course he would take: this afternoon he'd get off at Inchney, make his rounds until the stores closed, then get a ride in some way to Piffer's Road and spend the long summer evening making inquiries. If he recollected correctly from his map the distance between the large town and the tiny community was given as seven miles. At worst, he could walk back to Inchney in a couple of hours.

The first part proved even simpler than that. There was a bus, the clerk at the Inchney Hotel told him, that left at six o'clock.

At twenty after six, Caxton climbed off and, standing in the dirt that was Piffer's Road, watched the bus throb off down the highway. The sound faded into remoteness as he trudged across the railway track. The evening was warm and quiet, and his coat made a weight on his arm. It would be cooler later on, he knew, but at the moment he almost regretted having brought it.

There was a woman on her knees, working on the lawn at the first house. Caxton hesitated, then went over to the fence and stared at the woman for a moment. He wondered if he ought to remember her. He said finally, "I beg your pardon, madam."

She did not look up. She did not rise from the flower bed, where she was digging. She was a bony creature in a print dress, and she must have seen him coming to be so obstinately silent. "I wonder," Caxton persisted, "if you can tell me where a middle-aged man and his daughter live. The daughter is called Selanie, and she used to sell fountain pens and drinking cups and things to people on the train."

The woman was getting up. She came over. At close range she didn't seem quite so large or ungainly. She had gray eyes that looked at him with a measure of hostility, then with curiosity. "Say," she said finally, "weren't you along here about two weeks ago, asking about them? I told you then that they lived in that grove over there." She waved at some trees about a quarter of a mile along the road, but her eyes were narrowed as she stared at him. "I don't get it," she said grimly.

Caxton couldn't see himself explaining about his amnesia to this crusty-voiced, suspicious creature.

He said hastily, "Thank you very much. I—"

"No use going up there again," said the woman. "They pulled out on the same day you were there last time . . . in their big trailer. And they haven't come back."

"They're gone!" Caxton exclaimed.

In the intensity of his disappointment he was about to say more. Then he saw that the woman was staring at him with a faint, satisfied smile on her face. She looked as if she had successfully delivered a knockout blow to an unpleasant individual. "I think," Caxton snapped, "I'll go up and have a look around, anyway."

He spun on his heel, so angry that for a while he scarcely realized that he was walking in the ditch and not on the road. His fury slowly yielded to disappointment, and that in turn faded before the thought that, now that he was up here, he *might* as well have a look.

After a moment he felt amazed that he could have let one woman get on his nerves to such an extent in so short a time. He shook his head. He'd better be careful. The process of tracking down the projector—and his memory—was wearing on him.

A breeze sprang up from nowhere as he turned into the shadowed grove. It blew softly in his face, and its passage through the trees was the only sound that broke the silence of the evening. It didn't take more than a moment to realize that his vague expectations, the sense of . . . something . . . that had been driving him on this journey, was not going to be satisfied. For there was nothing, not a sign that human beings had ever lived here; not a tin can, not a bundle of garbage, no ashes from a stove. Nothing. He wandered around disconsolately for a few minutes, poked gingerly with a stick among a pile of dead branches. And finally he walked back along the road. This time it was the woman who called to him. He hesitated, then went over. After all, she might know a lot more than she had told. He saw that she looked more friendly.

"Find anything?" she asked with ill-restrained eagerness.

Caxton smiled grimly at the power of curiosity, then shrugged ruefully. "When a trailer leaves," he said, "it's like smoke—it just vanishes."

The woman sniffed. "Any traces that were left sure went fast after the old man got through there."

Caxton fought to hold down his excitement. "The old man!" he exclaimed.

The woman nodded, then said bitterly, "A fine looking old fellow. Came around first inquiring from everybody what kind of stuff Selanie had sold us. Two days later, we woke up in the morning and every single piece was gone."

"Stolen!"

The woman scowled. "Same thing as. There was a dollar bill for each item. But that's stealing for those kind of goods. Do you know, she had a frying pan that—"

"But what did he want?" Caxton interrupted, bewildered. "Didn't he explain anything when he was making his inquiries? Surely you didn't just let him come around here asking questions?"

To his astonishment, the woman grew flustered. "I don't know what came over me," she confessed finally, sullenly. "There was something about him. He looked kind of commanding-like and important, as if he were a big executive or something." She stopped angrily. "The scoundrel!"

Her eyes narrowed with abrupt hostility. She peered at Caxton. "You're a fine one for saying did we ask any questions. What about you? Standing there pumping me when all the time— Say, let me get this straight: *are* you the fellow who called here two weeks ago? Just how do you fit into the picture?"

Caxton hesitated. The prospect of having to tell his story to people like this seemed full of difficulties. And yet, she must know more. There must be a great deal of information about the month that the girl Selanie and her father spent in the district. One thing seemed certain. If any more facts were available, the woman would have them.

His hesitation ended. He made his explanation, but finished a little uncertainly: "So you see, I'm a man who is—well, in search of his memory. Maybe I was knocked over the head, although there's no lump. Then, again, maybe I was doped. *Something* happened to me. You say I went up there. Did I come back? Or what did I do?"

He stopped with a jump for, without warning, the woman parted her lips and let out a bellow. "Jimmy!" she yelled in an ear-splitting voice. "Jimmy! C'm'ere!"

"Yeah, Mom!" came a boy's voice from inside the house.

Caxton stared blankly as an uncombed twelve-year-old with a sharp, eager face catapulted out of the house. The screen door banged behind him. Caxton listened, still with only partial comprehension, as the mother explained to the boy that "this man was hit over the head by those people in the trailer, and he lost his memory, and he'd like you to tell him what you saw."

The woman turned to Caxton. "Jimmy," she said proudly, "never trusted those folk. He was sure they were foreigners or something, and so he kept a sharp eye on them. He saw you go up there, and most everything that happened right up to the time the trailer left. 'Course, it wasn't easy to know what went on inside, 'cause that whole big machine didn't have a single window in it. But," she finished, "he went inside once when they weren't around and looked the whole place over, just to make sure of course that they weren't pulling something."

Caxton nodded, suppressing his cynicism. It was probably as good a reason as any for snooping. In this case, it was lucky for him.

The thought ended, as Jimmy's shrill voice projected into the gathering twilight. . . .

The afternoon was hot, and Caxton, after pausing to inquire of the woman in the first house as to where the father and daughter lived, walked slowly toward the grove of trees that she had indicated.

Behind him, the train tooted twice, and then began to chuff. Caxton suppressed a startled impulse to run back and get on it. He realized he couldn't have made it anyway. Besides, a man didn't give up the hope of fortune as easily as that. His pace quickened as he thought of the print and the drinking cup, and the photo projector.

He couldn't see the trailer in the grove until he turned into the initial shady patch of trees. When he saw it, he stopped short. It was much bigger than he had pictured it even from Jimmy's mother's description. It was as long as a small freight car, and streamlined in that it actually tapered down a little at the rear.

No one answered his knock.

He thought the girl had run this way. . . . Uncertain, he walked around the monster on wheels. As Jimmy had reported, there were no windows; so it was impossible to see anywhere but up front where the driver's windshield and side windows showed a small view of two seats. Behind the second one there was a door leading into the main section of the trailer. The door was closed.

As far as he could discover, there were only two entrances, one on either side—a forward door on the far side, and a slightly rearward door where he had first approached the trailer.

Caxton returned to the door at which he had knocked and listened intently for sounds. But again there was nothing. Nothing, that is, except a thin wind that blew gently through the upper reaches of the trees. Far away the train whistled plaintively. He tried the latch, and the door opened so easily that his hesitation ended. Deliberately, he pushed it ajar and stood there staring into one of the rooms.

The first thing Caxton saw, as he climbed in, was the girl's basket standing against the wall just to the left of the door.

The sight stopped him short. He sat in the doorway, then, his legs dangling toward the ground. His nervousness yielded to the continuing silence and he began with a developing curiosity to examine the contents of the basket. There were about a dozen of the magic prints, at least three dozen of the folding, self-filling cups, a dozen roundish black objects that refused to respond to his handling, and three pair of pince-nez glasses. Each pair had a tiny transparent wheel attached to the side of the right lens. They seemed to have no cases; there seemed to be no fear that they would break. The pair he tried on fitted snugly over his nose, and for a moment he actually thought they fitted his eyes. Then he noticed the difference. Everything was nearer—the room, his hand—not magnified or blurred, but it was as if he were gazing through mildly powered field glasses. There was no strain on his eyes. After a moment, he grew conscious again of the little wheel. It turned quite easily.

Instantly, things were nearer, the field-glass effect twice as strong. Trembling a little, he began to turn the wheel, first one way, then the other. A few seconds only were needed to verify the remarkable reality. He had on a pair of pince-nez with adjustable lens, an incredible combination of telescope-microscope: super-glasses.

Almost blankly, Caxton put the marvelous things back in the basket. Then, with abrupt decision, he climbed into the trailer. He walked along a narrow corridor, first up front, and then to the rear, trying each door that he came to. There were eleven, and only two were unlocked. The first opened into a woman's small bedroom. A half-closed bureau showed women's things. Caxton gave the gleaming walls and ceiling of the interior one quick glance, noted the neatly-made fold-down bed, a shelf of books, and a chair; then guiltily he drew the door shut.

The remaining door that was unlocked led to the rear room. His first look into that showed the entire wall on one side fitted with shelves, each neatly loaded with a variety of small goods. Caxton picked up what looked like a camera. It was a finely made little instrument. He studied the lens; his fingers pressed something that gave. There was a click. Instantly a glistening card came out of a slit in the back. A picture.

It was of the upper part of a man's face. It had remarkable depth and an amazingly natural color effect. It was the intent expression in the brown eyes that momentarily made the features unfamiliar. Then he realized that he was looking at himself. He had taken his picture, and it had been developed instantly.

Astounded, Caxton stuffed the picture in his pocket, set the instrument down and, trembling, climbed out of the trailer and walked off down the road toward the village.

"And then," said Jimmy, "a minute later you came back and climbed in and shut the door and went toward the rear. You came back so fast that you nearly saw me; I thought you'd gone. And then . . ."

The trailer door opened. A girl's voice said something urgent that Caxton didn't catch. The next instant, a man answered with a grunt. The door closed and there was a movement and the sound of breathing.

"And that's all, mister," Jimmy finished. "I thought there was going to be trouble then. And I hiked for home to tell Mom."

"You mean," Caxton protested, "I was unlucky enough to come back just in time to get myself caught, and I didn't dare show myself?"

The boy said, "What I've told you is all I saw."

"That's all you know?"

Jimmy hesitated. "Well," he began finally in a defensive tone, "what happened then was queer. You see, I looked back when I got to the road, and the trailer wasn't there no more."

"Wasn't there?" Caxton spoke slowly. Mentally, he looked over the area as he had seen it, trying to visualize the action. "You mean, they started up the engine and drove to Piffer's Road, and so on down to the highway?"

The boy shook his head stubbornly. "Folks is always trying to trip me up on that. But I know what I saw and heard. *I* was on Piffer's Road. There weren't no sound of an engine. They was just gone suddenly, that's all."

Caxton felt an eerie chill along his spine. "And I was aboard?" he asked.

"You was aboard," said Jimmy.

The silence that followed was broken by the woman saying loudly, "All right, Jimmy, you can go and play now."

She turned to Caxton. "Do you know what I think?" she said.

With an effort, Caxton roused himself. "What?" he said.

"They're working a racket, the whole bunch of them together. The story about her father making the stuff. I can't understand how we fell for that. He just spent his time going around the district buying up old metal. Mind you"—the admission came almost reluctantly— "they've got some wonderful things. But there's the rub. So far, these people have only got hold of a few hundred pieces altogether. What they do is sell them in one district, then steal them back and resell them in another."

In spite of his intense self-absorption, Caxton stared at her. He had run across the peculiar logic of fuzzy-minded people before, but it always shocked him when facts were so brazenly ignored in order that a crackpot theory might hold water. He said, "I don't see where the profit comes in. What about the dollar you got back for each item that was stolen?"

"Oh," said the woman. Her face lengthened. Then she looked startled. And then, as she grasped how completely her pet idea had been wrecked, an angry flush suffused her wind- and sun-tanned face. "Some publicity scheme, maybe!" she snapped.

It struck Caxton that it was time to terminate the interview. He said hastily, "Do you know anyone going into Inchney tonight? I'd like to get a ride if I could."

The change of subject did its work. The high color faded from the woman's cheeks. She said thoughtfully:

"Nope, no one I know of. But don't worry. Just get on the highway, and you'll get a lift."

The second car picked him up.

VII

HE SAT IN the hotel as darkness fell thinking of the girl
and her father with a carload of the finest manufactured
goods in the world. She sells them as souvenirs, one to a
person. He buys old metal. And then, as added insanity,
an old man goes around buying up the sold goods—he
thought of Kellie's print—or destroying them. Finally,
there was the curious amnesia of a photo-supply salesman named Caxton, who had started out looking for the
origin of a certain projector.

Somewhere behind Caxton, a man's voice cried out in
anguish, "Oh, look what you've done now. You've torn
it."

A quiet, mature, resonant voice answered, "I beg your
pardon. You paid a dollar for it, you say? I shall pay for
the loss, naturally. Here—and you have my regrets."

In the silence that followed, Caxton stood up and
turned. He saw a tall, splendid looking man with gray
hair, in the act of rising from beside a younger man who
was staring at the pieces of a photoprint in his fingers.
The old man headed for the revolving door leading to
the street, but it was Caxton who got there first, Caxton
who said quietly but curtly, "One minute, please. I want
an explanation of what happened to me after I got into
the trailer of the girl Selanie and her father. And I
think you're the man who can give it to me."

He stopped. He was staring into eyes that were like

pools of gray fire, eyes that literally seemed to tear into his face, and to peer with undiminished intensity at the inside of his brain. Caxton had time for a brief, startled memory of what Kellie had said about the way this man had outfaced them on the train with one deadly look, and then it was too late for further thought. With a tigerish speed, the other stepped forward and caught Caxton's wrist. There was a feel of metal in that touch, metal that sent a tingling glow along Caxton's arm, as the big man said in a low, compelling voice, "This way—to my car."

Caxton barely remembered getting into a long, gleaming, hooded car. The rest was darkness—mental . . . physical. . . .

He was lying on his back on a hard floor. Caxton opened his eyes and for a blank moment stared at a domed ceiling two hundred feet above him. The ceiling was at least three hundred feet wide, and nearly a quarter of it was window, through which a gray-white mist of light showed, as if an invisible sun were trying hard to penetrate a thin but persistent fog.

The wide strip of window ran along the center of the ceiling straight on into the distance. *Into the distance!* With a gasp, Caxton jerked erect. For a moment then his mind wouldn't accept what his eyes saw.

There was no end to that corridor. It stretched in either direction until it became a blur of gray marble and gray light. There was a balcony and a gallery and a second gallery; each floor had its own side corridor, set off by a railing. And there were countless shining doors and, every little while, a branch corridor, each suggesting other vast reaches of that visibly monstrous building.

Very slowly, the first enormous shock over, Caxton climbed to his feet. Memory of the old man—and what had gone before—was a weight in his mind. He thought darkly: *He got me into his car, and drove me here.*

But why was he here? On all the wide surface of the Earth, no such building existed.

A chill went up his spine. It cost him a distinct effort to walk toward the nearest of the long line of tall, carved doors and pull it open. What he expected, he couldn't have told. But his first reaction was disappointment. It was an office, a large room with plain walls. There were some fine-looking cabinets along one wall. A great desk occupied the corner facing the door. Some chairs, and two comfortable-looking settees and another, more ornate door completed the picture. No one was in the room. The desk looked spick and span, dustless. And lifeless.

The other door proved to be locked, or else the catch was too complicated for him to operate.

Out in the corridor again, Caxton grew conscious of the intense silence. His shoes clicked with an empty sound. And door after door yielded the same office-furnished but uninhabited interior.

Half an hour passed, by his watch. And then another half hour. And then he saw the door in the distance. At first it was only a brightness. It took on glittering contours, became an emormous glass affair set in a framework of multitinted windows. The door was easily fifty feet in height. When he peered through its transparent panes, he could see great white steps leading down into a mist that thickened after about twenty feet, so that the lower steps were not visible.

Caxton stared uneasily. There was something wrong here. That mist, obscuring everything, persisting for hours, clinging darkly. He shook himself. Probably there was water down there at the foot of the steps, warmish water subjected to a constant stream of cold air, so thick fog formed. He pictured that in his mind, a building ten miles long standing beside a lake, and buried forever in gray mists.

Get out of here! Caxton thought sharply.

The latch on the door was at a normal height. But it was hard to believe that he would be able to maneuver the gigantic structure with such a comparatively tiny leverage. It opened lightly, gently, like a superbly balanced machine. Caxton stepped out into the pressing fog and began, swiftly at first, and then with developing caution, to go down the steps. No use landing up in a pool of deep water. The hundredth step was the last; and there was no water. There was nothing except mists, no foundation for the steps, no ground.

On hands and knees, dizzy with a sudden vertigo, Caxton turned around and started crawling up the steps. He was swaying so dizzily inside, like an untrained man who has suddenly been swung out over a cliff clinging to a rope, that he only caught a glimpse of the room in a sort of after-vision.

He had glanced back in his agony. It was entirely a chance movement of his head, a wobble of his body which made his neck roll loosely . . . and he saw the room.

Caxton stopped. But that, also, was an unmonitored act. The image flitted through his mind like a fantasy, and if he had had any strength that is all it would have been—a fantasy. If he had had any strength, he would have climbed on, and the scene would have faded as a dream fades. But he was gasping from the weakness of fear that had seized him; and he lay down full-length on that step, bracing himself there with his hands, one palm on the step below, the other on the one above.

When he was able to look there, through a chink in the fog, was the room. It was slantingly off to one side toward the farther reaches of the steps. But it was brightly lighted, and the drifting fog had an effect like a half-drawn curtain that somebody kept trying to close, and couldn't quite.

Exactly how long it took until he was over by that "curtain" Caxton never afterward remembered. He did not even recall his route. He must have crawled along one step to the point opposite the break in the fog, and then he must have gingerly lowered himself toward the half-open "curtain."

He presumed it was a crawling action. Because, surely, he wouldn't have dared to stand erect.

Besides, when he abruptly came to awareness, he was kneeling on the second step, and thinking that it was safer to operate from there.

Caxton eased his foot over from the step to the floor. What he expected was not clear, but what happened was that he touched a solid floor.

Even then it took a timeless period, again because he had no awareness, to decide to trust his weight to the floor.

I'm a schoolteacher type making like a steeplejack, he was thinking wanly. . . . Oddly, that picture of himself was calming.

He had a realization. The floor was holding him with the stable power of a genuine floor of a genuine room.

What had happened? He had pushed himself away from the steps, yet he held to them while he edged his body along the glossy smooth (plastic?) floor.

Abruptly, he stood up—and he was in the room.

That quick. That easy. And the ridiculous part was that, as he straightened, he saw a window in the room . . . and a scene beyond the window . . . and he forgot caution.

It was a moment of total forgetfulness. For the window was huge, and he could see what was beyond it.

For that moment, he was lost in wonder. He ran to the window like a child; and it was only as he was standing there that he realized how completely he had abandoned the automatic good sense of his prolonged over-stimulation—the kind of inner excitement that in the past he had always called temporary nervous breakdowns.

As he stood there, realizing that he had done it again, he was stunned by the deadliness of such a lapse . . . that if anything had gone wrong, it could have been the end for him to the exact extent of the wrongness.

The thought-feeling faded. He had never been a man who clung to past fears. His inner world was adaptive, and not normally given to might-have-beens. He could be thrown. How he could be thrown! His reaction at Tichenor Collegiate was but a sample of a lifetime of similar strong reactions. What had always saved him from such . . . breakdowns . . . was that he seldom introspected about them after they were over.

He didn't now.

There directly in front of him was the window. There was the scene outside the window. Automatically, he began to react to that.

VIII

HE WAS LOOKING out from a height at a city. Caxton caught his breath in a quick inhalation, because—

It was the city of the novelty films from the Arlay Library. The sky was dotted with Fly-O's. Thousands of them. But even the residential street—as he now perceived it to be—which this house overlooked, had people on the streets, just plain walking.

Except for the Fly-O's, he saw no vehicles during that first wondering look.

What he could see of the city was not obviously different from the many-storied megalopolitan monsters of his own time. There seemed to be more gleam, more sunlight reflection.

More glass? Caxton wondered. *Or, perhaps, transparent plastic?*

Those fleeting observations ran their respective courses. And it was then that he had his big thought: *What city? What year?*

Instantly, with that thought, he was in another of his breakdowns.

WHAT YEAR?

He whirled. He saw a door and he ran toward it. It opened to his touch, and beyond it were steps leading down to an ornate lower hallway, and to a big glass door that led outside to some outside steps. These took him down to the street.

As he went through a vaguely observed gate out onto what looked like a plastic sidewalk, a modicum of sense returned to Caxton.

I could get lost.

The excitement, the abnormal nervousness, remained. But after that realization, he was able to force himself to pause and to examine his surroundings. Here at street level he saw that the house from which he had almost catapulted himself was one of several on the highest level of a slope.

It was immensely reassuring. Hard to lose that.

All I want is one look at a newspaper. . . . The paper would have the date and the name of the city. He would snatch it up, take one look at it—and then he would rush back to the house and up to a room where a strange fog framed a passageway to some giant steps of a building through which he had come from another time.

Caxton grew aware that to his right, about a block distant, the buildings that he could see had the shape and silhouette of being a shopping center.

As he ran, he passed people who were dressed in brilliantly colored silken-like, loose-fitting slacks and coats. Over this, many that he saw wore matching colored Fly-O's, strapped to their backs around the shoulders and under the armpits.

It was the awareness of the difference in clothing between the others and himself that slowed Caxton down. He had the distinct feeling that a man in an outlandish, old-fashioned suit, should be walking.

He came to the shopping center with that restraining thought still holding him back from an impulse to run at top speed. There were no street vehicles on this busier street, either. But there were more people, his quick glance, it seemed to him, counted several hundred.

The scene was utterly fascinating. Every few moments, a man or woman with a Fly-O would swoop down from the sky, or take off from the sidewalk. . . . At first, Caxton held his breath each time. Each time the fear came that the person would fall back, or land too hard. But he presently saw that to those who were doing it, it was all so casual, and such a great number of individuals were involved, that abruptly his anxiety turned back on himself.

Again, it was his appearance that concerned him.

I must look strange, he thought.

But the truth was, people merely glanced at him and that brought him back to a variation of an old conviction: it was a big world; even back in the 1970's that had been so. Each human being had only twenty-four hours, and therefore was busy with his own purposes. The merely bizarre could not distract him.

I could be an actor coming from a rehearsal . . . How would they know? And why would they care? Back home, passersby never gave an oddball more than a glance.

It was the same here, and so he was free to gaze. The excitement that came then had no parallel in his previous experience. Here were the children of the children of the children of the people of his own time. . . . *My God, it's terrific!*

In that keyed-up state of exhilaration, he walked an entire block. He merely glanced into store windows, and into the open doors of shops. Several times, he had a vague impulse to stop and just stare at what he saw. But he couldn't even slow down from that rapid walk; his muscles moved him automatically forward.

But he did notice that the shops were not too different from his own era. And that did not surprise him. Shopkeepers and their goods had been an enduring aspect of man's world for thousands of years.

Nonetheless, the reality of it relieved Caxton. It was a familiarness that even absorbed some of his developing dismay at the fact that he saw neither newspapers nor magazines.

I'll have to ask somebody, he thought, highly disturbed. What was disturbing was that he couldn't imagine how he could present such a question.

All he wanted was the date: the day, the month, the year.

It seemed such a little thing. Yet Caxton had the distinctly unhappy conviction that people didn't answer questions like that. The day, yes. Like, you could say that you didn't know if this was the 22nd or the 23rd. But after they'd told you which, and you said, "Well, what month? And then when they'd give you a funny look, and told you—then you asked the big one: *What year?*

How would you ever know that the reply you got wasn't as facetious as the replier would assume your question to be.

With a conscious effort, Caxton stopped his gyrating mind and, entirely on instant impulse, walked over to a man who was standing gazing into a shop window just ahead. To this stranger, Caxton said, "Excuse me, sir."

The man turned. He had brown eyes, and his hair was combed thick, and it was dark brown. His face skin was smooth and pink, and he was younger than Caxton, seeming to be about thirty.

He said in perfectly plain, understandable English, "What's the matter? Are you ill?"

So I look wild. . . . Even as he had the realization, Caxton parroted the thought that had so abruptly moved him to this communication, "I seem to have amnesia. What year is this? Where am I? What city is this?"

The stranger gazed at him sympathetically, then he raised his arm. As he did so, part of the loose sleeve fell away from his wrist and hand, revealing a bracelet.

"Where's yours?" the man asked.

All in a flash, Caxton decided that the bracelet was an identification. In that same flash, he saw himself trapped by his single act of having spoken to one person.

He spun away, and headed across the street at a dead run. Looking hastily back, moments later, he saw that the man had not moved, was still standing there at the window. But he was gazing at Caxton.

Reassured, Caxton slowed. But after a moment he realized there was something about the other man that bothered him still: the *way* he was standing. He glanced back again and, though he was farther away now, there was no question. The fellow had his arm raised, and he was holding the bracelet on his wrist close to his mouth.

His mouth was moving.

Caxton had come to a corner. Abruptly terrified, he whipped around that corner and ran along the street that was there.

This time, as he ran, he had a new feeling: disorientation. It was a horrifying internal sensation. Somehow, he kept refusing to accept that the streets were really solid, permanent places. It was a complete madness. The feeling came that it wasn't he that was moving, but that the sidewalks were shifting on him. He recalled a similar experience as a boy, when, looking down at a stream from a bridge, suddenly it was the bridge that seemed to be moving.

Now it was not just the stream or a bridge, but the whole world that was moving. He realized that part of his turmoil came from the fear that he had ventured too far. Everything looked strange. It was as if he had got turned around.

I shouldn't have run like that.

He stopped, gulping with the terrible inner effort to regain self-control. And grew aware that a girl—she looked only about twenty—was standing a few feet away, gazing at him, wide-eyed. She said simply, "You're the man they're looking for. Wouldn't you like help?"

Caxton stared at her, his mind trying to grasp the horrifying idea that he had evidently been made the object of a general alarm.

He stammered, "Tell me the date, and what city this is."

"Why, of course." Her tone humored him." This is Lakeside, and it's June third, 2083 A.D. Does that help?"

Just like that, he had his information. And his luck continued. For even as she spoke, Caxton's glazed eyes accidentally stared past her over the low structure across the street—to a small shop. And there, just beyond, he could see a hill with some houses on it.

"Tell them I don't need help," Caxton said to the girl. "Thank you."

And he ran. Around a corner, a hundred feet away up a steeply climbing street, he raced, puffing. As he arrived at the gate of the house—his destination—he stood there, gasping for breath. And he glanced back. And up.

Several Fly-O's were bearing slantingly down toward him. . . . Caxton fumbled with the gate catch, and when it wouldn't give, he vaulted over the fence and so up the steep outside stairway. It was as he reached the glass (?) door that he paused again, and looked back. Seven Fly-O's—all men—had stopped outside the line of the yard, and were hovering about a hundred feet above him and an equal distance away.

"Are you all right?" one of them called.

"Yes."

"This is your home?"

"Yes."

"Very well."

Caxton didn't wait. He was trembling at the fineness of the timing that had brought him to safety on such a narrow margin. And, since he wasn't quite safe yet, he flung the door open, and he was inside before the thought struck him that suppose the door had been locked—what then?

By the time the repercussion of that had trembled its way through him, he was up the stairway. At the top he saw that there were several doorways, evidently leading to different rooms, and that brought its own brief disorientation. Yet in the end he headed unerringly to the correct one. The next second, the door closed behind him. And he was in *the* room.

Now, for the first time, he saw that from this side there was no fog. Simply, in one corner, was a kind of ragged tear in the wall. Beyond the opening thus created, he could see the great white steps that led to the vast building from which he had emerged earlier.

Mission accomplished! he thought jubilantly.

He felt no shame at the way it had been accomplished. No sense of having repeatedly disgraced himself by his out-of-control, almost totally unthinking behavior. He had always accepted his own madnesses. His big task—

always—had been to keep other people from finding out how unstable he was. And for a long time, now, he'd felt pretty smug about his success at *that*. Just imagine, little idiot Petie Caxton was now an M.A. in physics, and rapidly heading for the top of the heap. Proving, he had often thought, that you really could fool most of the people most of the time.

A variation of that self-reassuring thought was in his mind, as he edged his way through the jagged opening and onto the lower step beyond. Far from being anxious about how solid it or the others might be, he put his weight on it without pausing and ran all the way up to the huge door.

The door itself opened at his touch in the same easy, balanced fashion as when he had come out. He could almost have moved it with one finger.

Seconds later, he was inside the great building, safe, momentarily, at least—and with his next purpose already fully formed in his mind.

IX

It was time he explored the fantastic building. First, one of the offices. Examine every cabinet. Break open the desk drawers and search them.

It wasn't necessary to break anything. The drawers opened at the slightest tug. The cabinet doors were unlocked. Inside were journals, ledgers, curious-looking files. Absorbed, Caxton glanced through several that he had spread out on the great desk. Finally, he pushed everything aside but one of the journals. This he opened at random, and read the words printed there:

SYNOPSIS OF REPORT OF POSSESSOR
KINGSTON CRAIG IN THE MATTER
OF THE EMPIRE OF LYCEUS II
A.D. 7,346-7,378

Frowning, Caxton stared at the date; then he read on:

The normal history of the period is a tale of cunning usurpation of power by a ruthless ruler. A careful study of the man revealed an unnatural urge to protect himself at the expense of others.

TEMPORARY SOLUTION: *A warning to the Emperor, who nearly collapsed when he realized that he was confronted by an immortal Possessor. His instinct for self-*

preservation impelled him to give guarantees as to future conduct.

COMMENT: *This solution produced a probability world type five, and must be considered temporary because of the very involved permanent work that Possessor Link is doing on the fringes of the entire seventy-third century.*

CONCLUSION: *Returned to the Palace of Immortality after an absence of three days.*

Caxton sat there, stiffly at first, then he leaned back in his chair; but the same blank impression remained in his mind. There seemed to be nothing to think about the report. At last he turned a leaf, and read:

SYNOPSIS OF REPORT OF POSSESSOR
KINGSTON CRAIG

This is the case of Laird Graynon, Police Inspector, 900th Sector Station, New York City, who on July 7, A.D. 2830, was falsely convicted of accepting bribes, and de-energized.

SOLUTION: *Obtained the retirement of Inspector Graynon two months before the date given in the charge. He retired to his farm, and henceforth exerted the very minimum of influence on the larger scene of existence. He lived in this probability world of his own until his death in 2874, and thus provided an almost perfect 290A.*

CONCLUSION: *Returned to the Palace of Immortality after one hour.*

There were more entries, hundreds—thousands altogether in the several journals. Each one was a Report of Possessor Kingston Craig, and always he returned to the "Palace of Immortality" after so many days, or hours, or weeks. Once it was three months, and that was an obscure, impersonal affair that dealt with the *establishment of the time of demarcation between the ninety-eighth and ninety-ninth centuries* and involved *the resurrection into active, personal probability worlds of their own of three murdered men, named* . . .

What finally—progressively—bothered Caxton was, if these . . . Possessors (Possessors of what, for heaven's sake?) . . . returned to the Palace of Immortality *that often*, where were they?

On impulse, he walked out into the hallway, and stared along its silent distances. The utter stillness that fed back to him was startling. And he noticed something. It seemed to him that the place was dimmer. It was harder to see. Was it possible that night was falling? Suddenly, he pictured himself alone in this tomb-like building in pitch darkness, and the calm of the past several hours vanished. Anxiously, he made his way along the first side corridor that he could find, and, to his great relief, found a stairway going up.

Caxton bounded up the stairs and tried the first door he came to. It opened into the living room on a magnificent apartment. There were seven rooms, including a kitchen that gleamed in the dimming light, with built-in cupboards that were packed with transparent containers. The contents were foods that were both familiar and strange.

Caxton felt without emotion. Nor was he surprised as he manipulated a tiny lever at the top of a can of pears to have the fruit spill out onto the table, although the can had not opened in any way. He saw to it that he had a dish ready for the next attempt; that was all. Later, after he had eaten, he sought for light switches. But it was becoming too dark to see clearly.

The main bedroom had a canopied bed that loomed in the darkness, and there were pajamas in a drawer. Lying between the cool sheets, his body heavy with approaching sleep, Caxton thought vaguely of the girl Selanie and her fear of the old man, why had she been so afraid? And what *could* have happened in the trailer that had irrevocably precipitated Peter Caxton into this?

He slept uneasily, with the thoughts still in his mind.

The light was far away at first. It came nearer, grew brighter, and at first it was like any awakening. Then, just as Caxton opened his eyes, memories flooded into his mind. He was lying, he saw tensely, on his left side. It was broad daylight. From the corners of his eyes he could see, above him, the silvery-blue canopy of the bed. Beyond it, far above, was the high ceiling.

In the shadows of the previous evening he had scarcely noticed how big and roomy and luxurious his quarters were. There were thick-piled rugs and paneled walls and rose-colored furniture that glowed with costly beauty. The bed was of king-size, four-poster construction.

Caxton's thought suffered a dreadful pause because, in turning his head away from the left part of the room toward the right, his gaze fell for the first time on the other half of the bed. A young woman lay there, fast asleep. She had dark brown hair, a snowy-white throat, and, even in repose, her face looked fine and intelligent. She appeared to be about thirty years old. She bore a startling resemblance to Selanie, but was older.

Caxton's examination got no further. Like a thief in

the night, he slid from under the quilt. He reached the floor and crouched there. He held his breath in desperate dismay as the steady breathing from the bed stopped. There was the sound of a woman sighing, and finally doom!

"My dear," said a rich contralto voice, lazily, "what on earth are you doing on the floor?"

There was movement on the bed, and Caxton cringed in anticipation of the scream that would greet the discovery that he was not *the* "my dear." But nothing happened. The lovely head came over the edge of the bed. Gray eyes stared at him tranquilly. The young woman seemed to have forgotten her first question, for now she said, "Darling, are you scheduled to go Earthside today?"

That got him. The question itself was so stupendous that his personal relation to everything seemed secondary. Besides, he was beginning to understand in a dim way.

This was one of those worlds of probability that he had read about in the journals of Possessor Kingston Craig. Here was something that could happen to Peter Caxton. And somewhere behind the scenes someone was making it happen. All because he had gone in search of—among other things—his memory.

Caxton stood up. He was perspiring. His heart was beating like a trip hammer. His knees trembled. But he stood up, and he said, "Yes, I'm going Earthside."

It gave him purpose, he thought tensely, reason to get out of here as fast as he possibly could. He was heading for the chair on which his clothes hung when the import of his own words provided the second and greater shock to his badly shaken system.

Going Earthside! He felt his brain sag before the

weight of a fact that transcended every reality of his existence. Going Earthside from where? The answer was a crazy thing that sighed at last wearily through his mind: from the Palace of Immortality, of course, the palace in the mists, where the immortal Possessors lived.

He reached the bathroom. The night before, he had discovered in its darkening interior a transparent jar of salve, the label of which said: BEARD REMOVER—RUB ON, THEN WASH OFF. It took half a minute; the rest, five minutes longer. He came out of the bathroom, fully dressed. His mind was like a stone in his head, and like a stone sinking through water he started for the door near the bed.

"Darling?"

"Yes?" Cold and stiff, Caxton turned. In relief, he saw that she was not looking at him. Instead, pen in hand, she was frowning over some figures in a big ledger. Without looking up, she said, "Our time-relation to each other is becoming worse. I'll have to stay more at the palace, reversing my age, while you go to Earth and add a few years to yours. Will you make the arrangements for that, dear? Nineteen for me; you older by twice? Still true?"

"Yes," said Caxton, "yes."

He walked into the little hallway, then into the living room. Out in the corridor at last, he leaned against the cool, smooth, marble wall, and thought hopelessly: *Reverse her age!* So that was what this incredible building did! Every day here you were a day younger, and it was necessary to go to Earth to strike a balance.

The shock grew. Because what had happened to him in the trailer was so important that a superhuman organization was striving to prevent him from learning the truth. Somehow, today, he would really have to find out what all this was about, explore every floor, and try to locate some kind of central office. He was relaxing slowly, withdrawing out of that intense inward concentration of his mind when, for the first time, he grew conscious of sounds. Voices, movements, people below him.

Even as he leaped for the balcony balustrade, Caxton realized that he should have known. The woman there in the bed, where she hadn't been before had implied a world complete in every detail of life. But he felt shocked anyway. Bewildered, he stared down at the great main corridor of the building, along the silent, deserted reaches of which he had wandered for so many hours the day before. Now men and women swarmed along it in a steady stream. It was like a city street, with people moving in both directions, all in a hurry, all bent on some private errand.

"Hello, Caxton," said a young man's voice behind him.

Caxton had no emotion left for that. He turned slowly, like a tired man. The stranger who stood there regarding him was tall and well-proportioned. He had dark hair and a full, strong face. He wore a shapely one-piece suit, pleasingly form-fitting above the waist. The trouser part puffed out like breeches. He was smiling in a friendly, quizzical fashion. He said finally, coolly:

"So you'd like to know what it's all about? Don't worry, you will. Come with me. My name is Price, by the way."

Caxton held back. "What—" he began blankly. He stopped. His mind narrowed around the conviction that he was being rushed along too fast for understanding. This man waiting for him here at the door was no accident. He saw that Price was putting a glove on, and that he seemed to be having difficulty with it.

Caxton, watching him, relaxed a little, and said, "You stated that you wanted me to come with you. Where to?"

"I'm going to take you Earthside—your own era."

"You mean out of that big door, down those steps?"

"No, the other door," was the reply. "We'll ride there in one of the tubes below the main floor."

As he spoke, he finished pulling on the glove. He seemed a little breathless from the effort. Caxton noticed only vaguely. He was chagrined. The possibility of a basement transportation system had not occurred to him.

Nonetheless, he ceased his resistance. As Caxton walked beside the other, heading for the stairway, he realized that he was being extended a kind of friendliness. It bothered him, for he was a loner and did not have male friendships. He thought warily: *I won't leave this building, I won't go Earthside, or anywhere, until I understand everything.*

The biggest mystery to be explained, it seemed to him, was the condition of unoccupancy yesterday, and occupancy today.

They had reached the main corridor level; and now they started down another set of steps that Caxton hadn't noticed the evening before. He did not allow himself more than a moment's distraction, however, but asked his question.

The man replied, "We tried a couple of probability worlds on you, Caxton, to see how they fitted."

It seemed a meaningless concept. "You mean this?" Caxton asked. "Like my waking up beside an older Selanie as if I were married to her?"

"You are married to her in this probability world," said Price.

Caxton strove to visualize being married to the delightful girl he had seen on the train. He felt enthralled. Then, "But where was I yesterday? If that was yesterday."

"That was another probability time. Neither of them 'took,' I'm sorry to say."

The comment seemed threatening. "How do you mean?" Caxton spoke quickly.

"Well, in each one you remained yourself, and this last time we even worked it so it would be a probability for you about ten years younger. But the same rigid personality woke up. You'll agree, I'm sure, that you have no feeling of change. You are not involved, nor were you in what seemed to be yesterday."

"*Seemed* to be yesterday?" echoed Caxton.

"Well—"

Caxton interrupted, because he had another, bigger thought. "You mean I'm ten years younger?" His excited remembrance flashed back to the bathroom upstairs, where he had dressed. He had been in a disturbed state, but come to think of it—"Hey!" he said. "I remember when I looked in the mirror. I guess I did look younger."

"By ten years," said Price. "But it failed to change that tight personality structure." He broke off. "In here," he said.

They had come to an opening in a smooth, gray wall. It was an oval-shaped opening, and neatly fitted inside was a circular door, which was open. Caxton could see a row of seats in the lighted interior, and he deduced that this was the tube car that would transport them to an exit at the far end of this colossal building.

As he peered in, undecided about entering, Caxton hedged, "I'm sure I don't understand this probability stuff."

"It's not something that anyone understands," said

Price. "Selanie's father—Claudan Johns—who found the Palace of Immortality and this whole backfold in time, knows more about it than anyone else. But, like a scientist, what he has discovered are the laws, and undoubtedly not all of those, by which it operates. As a physicist you may be interested to know how extensive the phenomenon is."

He glanced questioningly at Caxton, who hesitated. Of all the things he didn't need at this moment was scientific information. He was trying to make up his mind where all this was leading. . . . *While I'm thinking, I'd better listen.*

And so he learned:

The universe was as time-vast as it was space-vast. In the same way that it proliferated galaxies by the billion, so it . . . permitted . . . probabilities, everywhere. It had happened that the conditions for creating a probability Earth other than the one that existed first, was that something from another time . . . an object, a person, was needed to break the pattern of energy that held that particular probability rigid. Actually, one object, or one person was not enough. Critical energy mass was involved. The best such masses were certain metallic compounds, known only to Possessor Johns. It was considered somewhat dangerous for a human being to be utilized for the purpose, because there was some kind of interaction between the energies involved and the object or person that was forcing the transformation. Hence, though it was theorized that a dozen Possessors deliberately joining together in a particular era could change that era, this had never been done. Instead, the metals were used.

Quite accidentally, there had been few, so far as could be determined, natural transfers from one era to another. Normally, the universe everywhere—or *almost* everywhere—moved forward through time at the slow, steady pace that, in the solar system, was measured in seconds, minutes, and hours. Presumably, there were other time foldbacks like the one in which the Palace of Immortality was hidden; but if Possessor Johns had a method for finding such foldbacks, he had not revealed that method to anyone. He *claimed* that he had stumbled on the foldback which now contained the Palace of Immortality as a result of an experiment he was conducting. But he had never explained what that experiment was.

"Basically," said Price, "there's very little to explain about the Palace of Immortality. It's located in a time foldback that goes along for several thousand years. It was already there when Claudan found it, and no one was in it, and there was no record of who built it."

Listening to the brief story, Caxton was struck by the name: Claudan Johns. The first name, Claudan, though obviously a simple development of an earlier word, had a futuristic sound to it. . . . It doesn't come from the twentieth century. Already, Caxton felt slightly ashamed at the thought, but the realization excited him.

Truth was the entire situation was fantastically impressive and exciting; and yet, after a few moments only, his mind focused on what Price had said about his rigid personality. "How should I have reacted?" he asked.

Price said, "Let me make our position very clear. Since you had tracked us down, and even had a run-in with our opposition—"

"That old man, you mean?" Caxton was instantly interested, "Opposition?" he asked. His voice went up. "You mean to tell me that with a good thing like this . . . Palace there's a schism?"

"It's very serious," was the reply. "Quite accidentally,

a paranoid acquired Possessor ability. Which means that he can go through time without using the Palace as an entry or exit, the way I still have to do, and Selanie, and of course you—"

"You're not a Possessor?" Caxton asked.

"No. I told you. I have to use the Palace. However, it's just one man, one mistake we made. Our hope is that the fantastic potential of endless probability—it seems infinite—will overwhelm it and him. What I was saying about you: we were willing for you to become associated with us. But—" He broke off. "Tell me, when did you become so worldly wise? Another word for it would be cynical. How young were you?"

"Oh"—Caxton put his mind back—"I was pretty sharp by the time I was fourteen. Caught my parents in bed around there. Boy! There they were pretending that no such thing as sex existed, and they were going at it like veterans. I would guess it was a complete disillusion-ment." He stopped. Again he had the feeling that he had been diverted to an unimportance by someone else's purpose. "Look," he protested, "this remarkable build-ing! It's unfair that you're keeping it to yourself."

"Don't worry," said Price, "we're not. We plan to pick up every human who ever lived before we're through."

"But people are dying," Caxton argued.

"They're available somewhere in their lifetime," was the answer. "We'll pick them up there, and they'll go on in some other probability world. We already have a lot of people helping us, as you saw. But we can always use more. That's why we gave you those two chances. But don't worry! We'll find you at an early age before you became disillusioned, and you'll go on in that prob-ability world. But I can tell you fourteen isn't it. How-ever, let's get started here."

"But—" Caxton frowned over the concept he had been offered. "What about me—*now?* What—?"

That was as far as he got. Price had stepped up beside him as if to assist him into the tube car. His gloved hand grasped Caxton firmly by the elbow. The shock that went through Caxton's body was exactly the same as when the old man had gripped the same elbow at the hotel.

There was a difference. That time, he had been caught by surprise. This time, he let out a yell and tried to jerk away. Or rather, he thought he yelled and thought he pulled back. The transition to vagueness and uncertainty was so swift that, after instants only, the only thing that was clear was that his elbow was held in a grip which seemed made of iron.

As from an enormous distance, Caxton heard Price say, "I'm sorry. We did our best for you. We were willing. But you weren't up to it. So what you get out of this is a ten-year rejuvenation treatment . . ."

The voice faded suddenly. There was a moment of darkness. And then—

Caxton blinked, and opened his eyes, and looked around at the street of a grubby little city that, with a growing sense of disaster, he recognized as Kissling. He was, he discovered, sitting on the curb directly in front of the hotel.

I'm back. Oh, damn, damn, damn!

X

THREE WEEKS WENT BY.

He was a salesman, who, since he needed the money, worked on commission (with advances) for the Quik-Photo Supply Corporation. And he had to cover his territory before returning to the home office.

He was a man with a certain aggressiveness, always accompanied by an ingratiating smile, and these things made for the elements of personality necessary to a salesman. What was more, he understood the basic science underlying every aspect of what he sold. In his travels, he ran into the kind of practical experts who operated photo-supply and development shops, often in conjunction with radio and TV service, and these, also, Caxton understood on a more fundamental level than his customers. It really helped his sales; for most practical experts were not above picking up bits of additional information about what they did.

But, finally, his sentence—his term on the road, as he regarded it—was served. Though his expense account allowed only for train fare, that was a delay he could not bear. He flew home, paying the difference out of his own pocket.

Since it was only about noon Friday when he got back, he had a free day—in fact, a free weekend—before having to check in at Quik-Photo. As he sat in the airport bus, his attention was completely concentrated on the fantastic experience he had had. And his thought was: How could he get back into the Palace of Immortality?

For three dribblingly slow weeks, he had been thinking of just that.

Caxton arrived at his room, and simply dropped his bags on the floor. He noticed the pile of mail his landlady had put on the table of his little kitchenette, but he couldn't even imagine anything there being of interest to him in his jumpy state of mind. Instead, he headed downstairs to his car, and drove straight to the storage company where he had hidden the stolen movie projector.

He couldn't find his deposit stub.

Scowling, he stood there in the office searching his billfold. It was irritating to realize that he must have left it in a billfold in another suit; and, since he was not a man who was timid, he finally gave the date of his coming here, and suggested that the clerk release the item without the stub.

The man was reluctant but not totally resistant. "If you can establish your identity . . ." he said, as he searched through a record book. Caxton located his driver's license, and then stood watching the seeking finger of the other probe through scores of pages. Finally, the old fellow paused. "Here we are," he said.

A frown shadowed his face. "I'm sorry, Mr. Caxton. These goods were picked up three weeks ago by someone who did have the stub."

The shock of that was with Caxton all the way home. The realization that they had traced him down brought the scary feeling that he was a marked man. He kept looking in his rear-view mirror to see if he was being followed, and he had the wild thought that maybe he could trace them by following his pursuer. But he saw no one.

Back in his little apartment, he read his mail, conscious that he was not reassured. His cheeks felt colorless: gray with fear, he realized. One of the letters he opened was from his attorney, and it contained a check for the large sum of two thousand, four hundred and thirty-two dollars. It required a long twenty seconds before Caxton was capable of appreciating that this was his share of what he had paid into a teachers' savings fund all these years. The rest, of course, had been forwarded to his divorcing wife as per the settlement.

Staring at the check, Caxton was conscious of some of his courage seeping back. He had always felt braver on payday. . . . *It's not,* he reasoned, *that it's such a great sum. Not these days.* . . . It wouldn't do, for example, to quit his job. But it gave him leeway. He had funds for extras in his search. Sitting there, he had another, more tremendous realization.

After all, they didn't kill me!

And they could have. No question, he had been totally at their mercy. Yet, it seemed now that all they wanted was to close the doors that he had opened, and to cut him off from what he had discovered. He surmised that they had found the stub in his pocketbook, and had somehow analyzed—or gotten out of him while he slept —what it was for.

Since they could have killed him, and hadn't, he decided that his fear was not rational. That line of reasoning was actually calming him, when he had another thought: *The films! Had they got to those, also?*

A minute later he was on the phone, shakily talking to Arlay, fighting once more to recover his self-control, and winning that fight as the voice at the other end assured him that, yes, the novelty films were still available. Though, of course, many of them were out on rental.

Caxton didn't waste any time. He rented a projector, and then drove to the Arlay Film Library and took all the films that Arlay had in stock. He spent the weekend endlessly replaying the incredible things: there were seven, including the one about how to repair a Fly-O and the one about how to repair a spaceship.

By late Sunday afternoon, a bleary-eyed Caxton knew exactly how to repair both items, but he had already experienced a sickening disappointment. Some of the repair items were integrated circuits. The circuits were labeled with letters and numbers, and were obtainable, the voice said, in any supply shop.

Available, though Caxton grimly, *from suppliers in the year 2083* A.D.

Nevertheless, he returned the films on Monday, and was happy to learn that two more had come back in the morning mail. Caxton rented them at once. As Arlay wrote up the rental transaction, Caxton grew aware that there was a pretty woman sitting in the back of the shop. Arlay must have become aware that Caxton had noticed her, for he straightened and introduced the woman as his wife, Tania.

Caxton's gaze met the woman's—and that was the beginning of his brief affair with Mrs. Arlay. At the moment, after that one quick interchange, in which she permitted him to exchange glances with her, it occurred to him that it had been a long time between women. Afterward, he tried to tell himself halfheartedly that he had decided in that instant that she might be useful to him in his purpose of obtaining prints of the novelty films from her husband.

They made love in his apartment within an hour of their meeting; there was no advance discussion. He had waited for her about half a block from the Arlay shop. She came there to the car within ten minutes. He asked her to follow him in her own auto, which she did. Such goodies had happened to him before. So he did not question the reason for them; simply accepted that some women—a few—were available on such terms. The fact that Tania Arlay was a very pretty woman with a well-made body was just his good luck this time. He hadn't always been that fortunate.

The act completed, they made arrangements to rendezvous again the next day whereupon she left hurriedly, and he sped down to the Quik-Photo head office, reporting in shortly after one o'clock.

The sales manager greeted him eagerly. "Like I told you on the phone this morning," he said, "some of these new item negotiations went through faster than I originally expected. So you're going to be around here for a couple of weeks, learning about them from manufacturers' reps. I advise you to spend time this afternoon just looking some of the stuff over, and figuring out questions you'd like to ask."

It seemed like a good suggestion—if he could put his attention on the problem at all.

All that first afternoon, while Caxton tried to concentrate, the chunky Bryson kept glancing in at him, or charging in from the front office to the back area, where Caxton worked, the indication being that he regarded as important what was going on there.

Abruptly, something of the older man's real purpose emerged. He burst out, "Caxton, you've got me puzzled. When I hired you, I thought of you as a man in his late thirties. But when you walked in here today, you looked like an overgrown kid. Damn it, you don't even look thirty."

"I lost some weight on the road," said Caxton. It was an explanation that he had made up in advance. "I am thirty-eight."

"Boy!" said the older man, "if losing weight can do that for somebody, I think I'll give up Danish cakes, ice cream, and liquor."

Caxton remained discreetly silent. He saw from the way the other's mind had been diverted that he had put over his point. . . . He thought smugly, *Naturally, what else could Bryson do but believe me?* The truth was totally incredible.

Tania Arlay, as a mistress, visibly showed the greatest contempt for the man who had married her. Twice during that week, she actually phoned Arlay from Caxton's bed. It seemed abnormal in a way that bothered Caxton—though he did not pretend to understand the rationale. He resolved within himself to make an end of the affair as soon as . . .

He had no clear decision, but certainly by the time he had seen all the films. . . . What brought the matter to a head was that Arlay suddenly refused to make further rentals to him. The notice of refusal came in the Friday morning mail, exactly one week after Caxton's return.

Caxton was instantly, guiltily convinced that Tania's husband had found out what was going on. Yet, as he anxiously reviewed the week and his relationship with her, he couldn't see how or when it could have happened. Thus convinced, he boldly went down and confronted Arlay.

The man was embarrassed, but presently he said frankly, sort of man to man, "I have to tell you this, Mr. Caxton. It was unfortunate that my wife was here last

Monday when you came in. She took a violent dislike to you, and to keep peace in my home I've discovered I have to refuse to do business with people she doesn't like."

So that was her method of camouflaging her misbehavior. Caxton mentally groped for a way that he might obtain a few more of the films, and finally said, "Look, I've still got three at home. How about trading me three more, and pretending on your books that they're the same ones? After that we can call off the transaction."

To this Arlay agreed reluctantly.

Later, when Caxton taxed the woman with her perfidy, she laughed her tinkling laugh, and said carelessly, "That's my way of handling my home situation. You can rent your films from someone else."

She took the attitude that the rental library had achieved its purpose in bringing them together.

So there he was after seven days with no direct access to the most remarkable films available in the twentieth century.

Cut off by his own impulse and false intuition. . . . *It's pretty bad,* thought Caxton grimly, *when you can't blame anyone but yourself.*

What now?

It had the look of the end of the trail. *I suppose,* he thought, *I could track down the fellow who had that camera shop in Kissling, from whom Quik-Photo had taken the movie projector as a trade-in.* The man had moved somewhere to the West Coast. Somewhere, vaguely.

Caxton began to feel vague himself.

He realized that reality consisted of accepting that it was all over, that life must go on in a drab way. Certain memories must be shunted into the realm of dim fantasies, to be considered occasionally, like interesting creations of an overstimulated imagination.

He settled himself for sleep on Friday night, reaffirming to himself that if that was what he must do, that was what he would do.

And woke up Saturday with a thought-feeling in his mind and body . . . such a thought as he had not had during the past month of turmoil; had never, in fact, had before in his practical life. Like a sharp, cutting instrument, it pierced to some deep and unsuspected yearning.

It brought a hope, oh—such a hope, such a thought!

The thought-feeling was that, since these people were immortal, through them—by forcing his way in—he could be immortal, also.

Incredibly, that precise purpose had not previously been a conscious, accepted possibility.

His logic now took him to the next step.

To reach them, he would have to cease all this fear, and this skulking, and find them—by whatever means. *Those nuts*, he thought scornfully, *thinking that some other version of me projected from an early age into another probability world, would be satisfactory.*

He had been having odd little dreams about it ever since. Images of himself, perhaps, having gone forward as a physicist and not as a teacher of physics. The picture was of a kind of simpler Caxton doing research earnestly, married to a strangely level-headed young woman—strange for him, he thought on those occasions when he visualized her, his own penchant being for a highly neurotic type of female.

The dream-image Caxton never seemed to notice the twisted world around him. At least, he didn't notice it with the critical concern that was a must if you really hoped to understand what a lousy place it was.

Ridiculous, thought Caxton. *It's me—the way I am right now—that's the one that's got to go forward.* He realized that he couldn't even imagine any other Peter Caxton being the "real" one.

So intense was his yearning, so strong his determination, that all the apathetic thoughts of the day before about how impossible his search was were gone almost as if they had never been.

He kept thinking: *I can go back to where I first saw Selanie. . . . There must be a clue.*

He drove to Piffer's Road that very day, arriving after a hard four hours' ride (and one speeding ticket) shortly after noon.

And found open countryside, brush, hill country. Nothing.

Returned to the city, shaken. A belief built up in him that his search had not been thorough. There were places he hadn't looked. . . . Rent a motorcycle, follow every trail.

Sunday, he went. His machine growled along back roads, forced into wooded areas, up streams.

Late that night, Peter Caxton, M.A. physicist, idled emptily back to his little one-room apartment in the city. And now, at last, he knew his problem.

How do you go a hundred-odd years into the future . . . if you absolutely have to?

. . . Have to, have to, have to—

The mental picture he saw was of himself emerging from the time eddy . . . shortly before noon, June 3, 2083 A.D.

If *he* could be waiting there near that house at the moment when his . . . earlier . . . self went off to that shopping center; and if he could then go into the Palace of the Possessors, and hide—

What he would do there was a little obscure. But he visualized himself *this time* making a study of the whole situation, a proper scientific study, for which he would prepare himself, for which, in fact, he was already partially prepared . . . from the films he had studied.

There's got to be a way, Caxton told himself obstinately.

During the three nothing days that followed, he never for a moment lost that feeling of obstinacy.

XI

THE WAY revealed itself on the fourth morning.

Caxton opened the morning paper, and read the headline: 500-YEAR SPACE TRIP.

The subhead stated: "James Renfrew to sponsor fantastic voyage to Alpha Centauri. Will go along himself, says nationally known playboy millionaire."

The story under the subhead reported that four men would make the incredible journey. In addition to Renfrew, there would be Ned Blake, who was Renfrew's personal manager; and the Nobel-prizewinning chemist, Arthur Pelham, who was the inventor of the drug that made it possible for living creatures to be placed in suspended animation.

The newspaper account stated that the fourth member of the expedition had not yet been selected. Wanted was a Ph.D physicist, who would be the technical and scientific expert of the group in that field. Unfortunately, the paper quoted Ned Blake, "We have so far had turndowns from every physicist we have approached."

The news story continued, "However, the committed trio is confident that somewhere in the country is a qualified physicist who—"

At that point, Caxton dropped the paper and grabbed for the phone. It took a while, but in due course he obtained a number in New York. He dialed that number and gave his name and his purpose to the young woman who answered.

93

He was put through at once to a firm-voiced man who identified himself as Ned Blake. Blake questioned him closely, and with a developing friendliness and—could it be?—relief. He said finally, "We need a qualified physicist so badly, Mr. Caxton, that I'm sure we can make do with an M.A. What you have said sounds great to me. So why don't you fly to New York this afternoon? Your air ticket will be waiting at your airport office. When you get to New York, you'll be paged, and taken to—"

He gave the address of an office building in downtown New York, finished, "I'll leave your name with the guard on the thirtieth floor, and you can come up from there."

Caxton did not contact Quik-Photo. The question of what he could give as an excuse was too much for him. . . . *If nothing comes of it,* he thought, *I'll return here tomorrow, and brazen it through, somehow.*

But he had a feeling, a lifting feeling, a sense of soaring feeling, that this thing had the sound of steel and fire.

He was met at the New York airport by a chauffeur-driven Rolls-Royce. Caxton sat in the luxurious back seat feeling breathless all the way into town. It was excitement of a different kind; not fear. The thought, over and over, was that any appearance of courage and boldness takes you further up the scale of life.

It made him feel a lot better. Because in his own horrible-reacting fashion, he was being extremely brave. *Driven is the word,* he thought shakily.

At the thirtieth floor, after the guard had checked him through, he took a self-service elevator up several floors —and stepped out into a magnificent office. As he came gingerly forth from the elevator, three men, who had been sitting with glasses in their hands, put the glasses down and stood up.

Two of the three were heavily moustached, and wore their hair long but elegantly styled. The third man was well-dressed but conservatively. He was older, and almost bald.

One of the moustachioed men came forward, his hand out. He was square of jaw; his eyes were slightly narrowed, and there was just the edge of disappointment in his manner.

"Ned Blake," he said.

"Peter Caxton," said Caxton.

"You're younger than I thought, from our phone conversation," said Blake, and it was obvious from the tone of his voice that that was what disturbed him.

"I'm thirty-eight," said Caxton. "I taught high school physics for more than twelve years, which I can prove. . . . I'm sorry I look so young."

Actually he wasn't sorry at all . . . For heaven's sake, that was why he had come.

Before Blake could make a further comment, the other moustachioed man said, "Hell, Ned, he wouldn't be here if he didn't have some lingering youth in his cells."

Blake had, in fact, already relaxed. Now he eagerly grasped Caxton's wrist, and drew him toward his companions—first, to the conservatively dressed individual.

"This is Mr. Pelham, Mr. Caxton."

Caxton shook hands with the world-famous chemist, thinking, *I'm really up in the stratosphere, meeting a man like this.*

Aloud, he said, "Your great achievement makes this journey possible, sir, I realize."

Pelham was lean, leaner than he had looked in the newspaper photograph, his face almost angular in its thinness. He took Caxton's palm in his bony hand, and said in an intense tone, "As we told the papers, we want the physicist to be the first to awaken. What do you think? Are you capable of facing return to consciousness fifty years from now, when the other three of us are still in suspended animation?"

There was a muffled sound from the third man at this point. Then: "My God, Pelham, what a lousy introductory sentence!"

"No worse than Caxton's," said Pelham with a smile.

They were clearly on very intimate terms, for at this point the third man grabbed the chemist around the shoulders, and, leaning over and past the slight-built Pelham from several inches of greater height, grabbed Caxton's hand.

"I'm Renfrew," he said.

The newspaper had said that Renfrew was thirty-nine. He looked somewhat older. There were lines of dissipation in his cheeks, tiny red-purple streaks, and the beginning of puffiness. But he had the bluest eyes that Caxton had ever seen.

"We want to ask you a lot of questions," said Renfrew. "But we can do that on the way to the house where you'll be staying. In the morning, we'll call in the newspaper boys." The "house" to which they took him was a five-story mansion overlooking the East River. From his bedroom window, Caxton watched the river traffic for a while, and then finally gave in to exhaustion.

That was about five o'clock in the morning.

At noon the next morning what seemed to be at least a hundred news cameras flashed at Caxton. Some of the microphones that he spoke into, it developed, were TV and radio on national hookups.

It was while he and the others were being interviewed

that he heard Ned Blake say, in answer to a question, that he would have a thousand-dollar-a-week drawing account, and before takeoff would be given a hundred thousand dollars to assign to any dependents or relatives he wished.

Like a dream.

From that moment on, he was in that house, or in a Cadillac, or a Rolls-Royce, or in a magnificent office, or in Renfrew's private jet. . . . Several times, Caxton flew down with the others to Cape Kennedy, where the take-off would be, because of course with so much money and influence at work, the journey was in fact a combination government-private industry project.

He learned that Renfrew had coasted through a college engineering course; the man actually had retained a good portion of his training and was, scientifically, easy to talk to. Caxton quickly found that he himself was now also subject to Renfrew's warmth. The millionaire playboy had an amazing capacity for camaraderie. The first time Renfrew introduced him as "My dear friend, Peter," Caxton was electrified. He felt an instant response, an immediate desire to be worthy of such a friendship.

But afterwards, he cautioned himself . . . *Got to watch that. Don't get enmeshed in personal attachments.*

After all, I'm the guy that's going to turn this ship back when I wake up. And be on Earth again a couple of years before 2083 A.D.

Caxton had a number of moments of curiosity, as he watched the brilliant scene around him. He knew why *he* was going on this fabulous journey. But what would make a man like Renfrew bow out of a world where he had everything?

It was a question that, one day, he asked Blake. That

rather grim young man stared at him, and then shrugged, and said, "He says he's made love to four hundred beautiful women, eaten thousands of perfectly cooked steaks, played golf in the low seventies, shot a tiger and a lion—and wished he hadn't, because the damned things cried as they were dying. But that made him wonder about his own future. For him, a perfect universe, with millions of dollars, and servants for every purpose . . . except that each birthday he was a year older, and one day reasonably soon he would be eaten by worms. He figures that five hundred years from now, they may have solved the problems of life prolongation."

So it was the same reason. Caxton felt a special excitement. Oddly, it was validation. In the wee hours, he had had doubts about his own sanity . . . how crazy could you get?

But they were brief doubts, somehow. And having discovered that the same intense motive was now driving another man, they became more fleeting still.

It's truth, he thought. *There's nothing here for anybody.* . . . And out of nowhere an opportunity had come his way, and he was pursuing it with the singleness of purpose that had always driven him; only, now, an accident had taken him off one track and put him on another.

Blake, Caxton realized presently, liked him. More and more as departure time drew near, Blake sought him out, and Caxton learned more and more about Renfrew.

Blake was worried about his friend. "All that golden personality," he said in a low-voiced aside to Caxton on still another day, "is dependent on a lifetime of being a money king. . . . When he wakes up the first time out there in empty space and suddenly realizes that that isn't there any more . . ." Blake shook his head doubtfully, and his rugged square face showed grave concern, as he concluded, "What will happen is anybody's guess."

Caxton's thought was that the problem might not be as severe as Blake anticipated. Because, by the time Renfrew awakened—after a hundred years—the ship would be back in the solar system. . . . Naturally, Caxton made no mention of these reassuring thoughts.

The takeoff, when it finally came, was routine, of course.

XII

CAXTON AWAKENED with a start, and thought: *How was Renfrew taking it?*

He must have moved physically, for blackness edged with pain closed over him. How long he lay in that agonized faint, he had no means of knowing. His next awareness was of the throbbing of an engine.

Slowly this time, consciousness returned. He lay very quiet, feeling the weight of his years of sleep, determined to follow the routine prescribed so long ago by Pelham.

He didn't want to faint again.

He thought: *It was silly to have worried about Jim Renfrew. He wasn't due to come out of his state of suspended animation for another fifty years.*

He began to watch the illuminated face of the clock in the ceiling. It had registered 23:12; now it was 23:22. The ten minutes Pelham had suggested for a time lapse between passivity and initial action was up.

Slowly he pushed his hand toward the edge of the bed. *Click!* His fingers pressed the button that was there. There was a faint hum. The automatic massager began to fumble gently over his naked form.

First it rubbed his arms; then it moved to his legs, and so on over his body. As it progressed, Caxton could feel the fine slick of oil that oozed from it working into his dry skin.

A dozen times he could have screamed from the pain of life returning. But in an hour he was able to sit up and turn on the lights.

The small, sparsely furnished, familiar room couldn't hold his attention for more than an instant. He stood up.

The movement must have been too abrupt. He swayed, caught the metal column of the bed, and retched discolored stomach juices.

The nausea passed. But it required an effort of will for him to walk to the door, open it, and head along the narrow corridor that led to the control room.

He wasn't supposed to so much as pause there, but a spasm of absolutely dreadful fascination seized him, and he couldn't help it. He leaned over the control chair and glanced at the chronometer.

It said: *53 years, 7 months, 2 weeks, 0 days, 0 hours and 27 minutes.*

Fifty-three years! A little blindly, almost blankly, Caxton thought of the people they had known back on Earth, the young men they had gone to college with, that girl who had kissed him at the party given them the night they left—they were all dead. Or dying of old age.

Caxton remembered the girl very vividly. She was pretty, vivacious, a complete stranger. She had laughed as she offered her red lips, and she had said, "A kiss for the young one, too."

She'd be a grandmother now—or in her grave.

As he had these thoughts he began to heat the can of concentrated liquid that was to be his first food. Slowly, his mind calmed.

Fifty-three years and seven and one half months, he thought drably. Nearly four years over the allotted time. He'd have to do some figuring before he took another dose of Eternity drug. Twenty grains had been calculated to preserve his flesh and his life for exactly fifty years.

The stuff was evidently more potent than Pelham had been able to estimate from his short-period advance tests.

He sat tense, narrow-eyed, thinking about that. Abruptly, he grew conscious of what he was doing. Laughter spat from his lips. The sound split the silence like a series of pistol shots, startling him.

But it also relieved him. Was he actually being critical?

A miss of only four years was bull's-eye across that span of years. The method wasn't as simple as at the Palace of Immortality. But it worked, also.

He was alive and still young. Time and space had been conquered, by a second system of bypassing the years.

Caxton ate his soup, sipping each spoonful deliberately. He made the small bowlful last every second of thirty minutes. Then, greatly refreshed, he made his way back to the control room.

This time he paused for a long look through the plates. It took only a few moments to find Sol, a very brightly glowing star in the approximate center of the rearview plate.

Alpha Centauri required longer to locate. But it shone finally, a glow point in a light-sprinkled darkness.

Caxton wasted no time trying to estimate their distances. They *looked* right. In fifty-four years they had covered approximately one-tenth of the four and one-third lightyears to the famous nearest star system.

As Caxton straightened up, he realized that there was a thought in his mind, other than the one he was supposed to have at this point.

He was supposed to check on his three companions; make sure all was well with them.

He found himself resisting that; found himself thinking: *First, turn the ship around. Start the long journey back. It would be utterly ridiculous if, because of any delay now, the spaceship returned to Earth after June 3, 2083. . . . Have to remember, there was already a four-year overtime balance to compensate for.* He had originally estimated that it would require the equivalent of an Earth-day to make the turnabout and insure that the return course was exactly right.

Start that, then look.

As he sat there, making his precise calculations and setting the dials, he realized that he was irritated that he had, as his first reaction on awakening, been concerned about Renfrew.

That guy almost got to me, he thought. "*My dear friend, Peter*" indeed. *Damn it, he scarcely knew me when he said that. So it had to be a lie. Showed how easily influenced people were by wealth.*

Even I, thought Caxton tolerantly. . . . After a little, he realized that the "even I" was phony. Money had always been supremely important to him. Or rather, success had.

So the colossal success and wealth of the Renfrew family had made an enormous impact. In his thoughts, the man seemed bigger than life, as if somehow what happened to him was more important than what happened to Peter Caxton.

Which, of course, was ridiculous.

But it occurred to him, for the first time in all his years, that this was the feeling that must have motivated guards of ancient kings to sacrifice themselves, and die smiling with gladness that they had been able to be of service to the superbeing, the monarch.

Well, Mr. Renfrew was going to have the surprise of his pampered life when he awakened, and realized that his "dear friend" had turned the vessel back toward Earth.

It took him about an hour to make the initial reset. As he had it worked out, the ship would go into a shallow, curving turn, and, after approximately twelve hours, would be headed back toward Earth.

Caxton sat in the control chair, and waited for the tiny tug that would indicate that the small light-motors were doing their job. . . . It needed only a little push for a rocketship to change course in space.

Half an hour went by; and he felt nothing.

He checked his figures and the dials. The needles recorded that the miniature drives were working.

But he felt nothing. There was no sensation at all.

The vessel continued its endless forward coasting motion. Its speed was augmented only by a series of small light-motors, which were designed to increase the forward impetus by one foot a second every three minutes.

Almost infinitesimal, virtually imperceptible. But in deep space, that miniscule acceleration added to the enormous velocity attained by the machine on takeoff had, as anticipated, brought the craft to a satisfactory high speed at almost no cost in fuel. It was intended that at the halfway mark, the rear light-motors would cease operation, and similar engines in the front would start the slow reversal of the process.

Another hour went by. Still nothing.

Caxton was a badly worried man, when he suddenly had a shocking realization: *Those so-and-so's. I'll bet they expected this . . . I'll bet the controls are disconnected, so nobody can turn around.*

It occurred to him now, belatedly, that if his insight was true, there would be written information to that effect in the logbook. In a few moments he had the book, had it opened, and was gazing palely down at Pelham's fine, almost calligraphically beautiful handwriting.

All that he had feared was there in back and white. He read:

Dear Peter:

Of course, it has been our hope that as you read this, you are feeling in good spirits, eager to go forward to the great adventure ahead. But just in case some kind of panic has got hold of you—you'll agree, this would be a perfect moment for a real case of agoraphobia (fear of large spaces)—and, just in case that has happened, Jim, Ned, and I agreed that we would have to protect ourselves from any impulse on anyone's part to return to Earth during the first half of the journey. So, Peter, I have to tell you that a concealed computer—one that is solidly welded in under the floor—is programmed to compensate for any alteration in direction. Our reasoning is that after 250 years, it will take as long to get back as to go forward, and so, since we'll have to return to manual controls somewhere, that's the point.

Goodbye for the present, my friend. As you know, I administered the drug to you, then to Jim, then to Ned, and I shall now, finally, do it to myself. So I'm writing this in a world of space where I am as alone in my time as you are in yours. You three are

*deep in your long sleep, and I shall now join you
there.* Au revoir *and*

> Love,
> Arthur

Caxton reread the message; and his first reaction was
a sarcastic rejection of the endearment that ended it.
"Love," hell!

You so-and-so, he cursed Pelham. *You've just ruined
my life. . . .* That kind of love he could do without,
thank you.

The grim impulse toward bitter sarcasm passed.

Suddenly, the appalled realization hit him that he
would now have to go ahead with the original purpose
of the journey. Caxton felt an awful sinking sensation,
and then—just like that—a strong anxiety. It struck him
with a pang that he had been using up precious oxygen,
acting as if it would not be needed later.

He climbed shakily to his feet. . . . *Get back to sleep!*
he ordered himself. Blankly, he headed for his little
room. And he was actually sitting there with the needle
ready on the bedside set of built-in drawers, when he
remembered the others.

Slowly, he stood up again, realizing that he must do
his duty. Look in on them. Make his entries in the logbook. Conceal what he had tried to do. Protect himself.

Take them in a row, he thought. Pelham first.

As he opened the airtight door of Pelham's room, a
sickening odor of decayed flesh tingled in his nostrils.
With a gasp, he slammed the door, and stood there in
the narrow hallway, shuddering.

After a minute, there was still nothing but the reality.
Pelham was dead.

He was a man, standing there, who was now committed to a five-hundred-year journey in space. And the terror that seared through him had the awful thought that he would have to make that journey alone.

His next awareness was that he was running. He flung open Renfrew's door, then Blake's. The clean, sweet smell of their rooms, the sight of their silent bodies on their beds, brought a measure of sanity back to Caxton.

It was a moment for an emotion that he had never had before in his adult life: grief. Incredibly, he felt a warm wetness on his cheeks.

I'll be damned, he thought. *Me, crying.*

Still weeping, he went to the storeroom, and procured his personal spacesuit and a tarpaulin. But even with that help, it was a horrible business. The drug had preserved portions of the body, but pieces kept falling off as he lifted it.

At last, he carried the tarpaulin and its contents to the airlock, and shoved it into space.

After cleaning up, he went to the radio. It had been calculated that half a lightyear was the limit of radio reception, and they were very close to that limit. Hurriedly, though carefully, Caxton wrote his report out, then read it into a transcription record, and started sending. He set the record to repeat a hundred times.

In a little more than five months, headlines would be flaring on Earth.

He counted out fifty-five grains of Eternity drug, and dissolved them in the fluid provided. That was as close as he could get to the amount he felt would be required for one hundred and fifty years. He injected the dosage in five separate operations.

In the moments before sleep came, Caxton found himself thinking about Renfrew and about the terrible shock that he would experience, on top of all the natural reactions to a deep space situation that Blake feared he would feel.

Caxton tried to fight off the thought, strove to recapture a more personal feeling for himself and what he wanted.

But the worry about Renfrew was still in his mind when darkness came.

XIII

ALMOST INSTANTLY, he opened his eyes. He lay thinking: *The drug! It hadn't worked.*

The draggy feel of his body warned him of the truth. He lay very still, watching the clock overhead. This time it was easier to follow the routine except that, once more, he could not refrain from examining the chronometer as he passed through the galley.

It read: *201 years, 1 month, 3 weeks, 5 days, 7 hours, eight minutes.*

He sipped his bowl of that super soup, then went eagerly to the big logbook.

It was utterly impossible for Caxton to describe the thrill that coursed through him as he saw the familiar handwriting of Blake, and then, as he read what Renfrew had written. It was a report; nothing more: gravitometric readings, a careful calculation of the distance covered, a detailed report on the performance of the engines, and, finally, an estimate of speed variations, based on the seven consistent factors.

It was a splendid mathematical job, a first-rate scientific analysis. But that was all there was. No mention of Pelham, not a word of comment on what Caxton had written or on what had happened.

Renfrew had awakened; and, if his report was any criterion, he might as well have been a robot.

Caxton knew better than that.

So, Caxton saw as he began to read Blake's report, did Blake.

Peter:
   TEAR THIS SHEET OUT WHEN YOU'VE READ IT!
   Well, the worst has happened. We couldn't have received from fate an unkinder setback. I hate to think of Pelham being dead. What a man he was, what a friend! But we all knew the risk we were taking, he more than any of us. So all we can say is, "Sleep well, good friend. We'll never forget you."
   But Renfrew's case is now serious. After all, we were worried, wondering how he'd take his first awakening, let alone a bang between the eyes like Pelham's death. And I think that the first anxiety was justified.
   As you and I know, Renfrew was one of Earth's fair-haired boys. Just imagine any one human being born with his combination of looks, money, intelligence. His great fault was that he never let the future trouble him. With that dazzling personality of his, and the crowds of worshipping women and yesmen around him, he didn't have much time for anything but the present.
   Realities always struck him like thunderbolts. That goodbye party was enough to put anyone into a sort of mental haze when it came to realities. To wake up a hundred years later, and realize that those he loved had withered, died and been eaten by worms —well!
   (I deliberately put it as baldly as that, because the human mind thinks of awfully strange angles, no matter how it censors speech.)

I personally counted on Pelham's acting as a sort of psychological support to Renfrew; and we both know that Pelham recognized the extent of his influence over Renfrew. That influence must be replaced. Try to think of something, Peter, while you're charging around doing the routine work. We've got to live with that guy after we all wake up at the end of the five hundred years.

Tear out this sheet. What follows is routine.

Ned.

Caxton burned the letter in the incinerator, examined the two sleeping bodies—how deathly quiet they lay—and then returned to the control room.

In the plate, the sun was a very bright star, a jewel set in black velvet, a gorgeous, shining brilliant.

Alpha Centauri was brighter. It was a radiant light in that panoply of black and glitter. It was still impossible to make out the separate suns of Alpha A, B, and Proxima, but their combined light brought a sense of awe and majesty.

Well, he thought, *here I am on this fantastic trip; and simultaneously trying to not be on it. . . .* He realized the internal conflict. He was fighting excitement, and fighting being involved. The excitement came from the obvious fact that he was involved.

Perhaps, as Blake was urging, he even ought to worry about Renfrew. Yet, though he realized the glory of this trip—here they were, the first men to head for far Centaurus, the first men to aspire to the fixed stars—though he realized all that, somehow, he clung to his own purpose.

He told himself that the immense time involved was too meaningless for emotion. Better stick to his own goals; never forget that he was Peter Caxton who knew exactly—well, almost—what he was doing.

He did his work, took his third dose of the drug, and went to bed. The sleep found him still without a plan about Renfrew.

His third awakening was routine, except that as he read the logbook, he saw there was no Renfrew entry at all. And Blake's entry showed that Blake didn't know what to make of *that*, but he was intensely worried.

"At least," Blake wrote, "he gave himself the correct dosage, because I counted the capsules. Think hard, Peter, and destroy this note, also."

Later, as Caxton lay waiting for the final dosage of the trip to take effect, he thought: *What am I supposed to think?* If Renfrew really went off his rocker, they'd undoubtedly have to do something about it. But it would be Renfrew's problem, basically.

Nonetheless, he was aware of a tension in his body. Which he regretted, because on another level it was kind of exciting to think: *This is it. This time when I awaken, we'll be there.*

Something of that excitement must have bridged that final 150 years of time. Because, when Caxton awakened, he thought: *We're here! It's over, the long night, the incredible journey. We'll all be seeing each other, and seeing the great Centaurus suns.*

The strange thing, it struck him as he lay there exulting, was that the time seemed long. And yet . . . yet he had been awake only three times, and only once for the equivalent of a full day.

In the truest sense of meaning, he had seen Blake and Renfrew—and Pelham—no more than a day and a half ago. He had had only thirty-six hours of consciousness since takeoff.

Then why this feeling that millennia had ticked by, second on slow second? Why this eerie, empty awareness of a journey through fathomless, unending night?

Was the human mind so easily fooled?

It seemed to Caxton, finally, that the answer was that he had been alive for those five hundred years, all his cells and his organs had existed, and it was not even impossible that some part of his brain had been horrendously aware throughout the entire unthinkable period.

And there was, of course, the additional psychological fact that he knew now that five hundred years had gone by, and that—

He saw with a start that his ten minutes were up. Cautiously, he turned on the massager.

The gentle, padded hands had been working on him for about fifteen minutes, when his cabin door opened, the light clicked on, and there stood Blake.

The too-sharp movement of turning his head to look at the other man made Caxton dizzy. He closed his eyes, and heard Blake walk across the room toward him. After a minute, he was able to look at Blake again without seeing blurs. Caxton saw then that Blake was carrying a bowl of the soup. He stood staring down at Caxton with a strangely grim expression.

At last his countenance relaxed into a wan smile. " 'Lo, Peter," he said. "Ssssh!" he hissed immediately. "Now, don't try to speak. I'm going to start feeding you this soup while you're still lying down. The sooner you're up, the better I'll like it."

He was grim again, as he finished, almost as if it were an afterthought; "I've been up for two weeks." He sat down on the edge of the bed, and ladled out a spoonful of soup. There was silence then, except for the rustling sound of the massager. Slowly, strength flowed through Caxton's body; and with each passing second he became more aware of the grimness of Blake.

"What about Renfrew?" he managed, finally, hoarsely. "He awake?"

Blake hesitated, then nodded. His expression darkened with a frown; he said simply, "He's mad. He's stark, staring mad. I had to tie him up. I've got him now in his room. He's becoming quieter, but at the beginning he was a gibbering maniac."

"Are you crazy?" Caxton whispered at last. "Renfrew was never so sensitive as that. The mere passage of time, abrupt awareness that all his friends are dead, couldn't make him go insane."

Blake was shaking his head. "It isn't only that, Peter." He paused, then, "Peter, I want you to prepare your mind for the greatest shock it's ever had."

Caxton stared up at him with an empty feeling inside. "What do you mean?"

Blake went on, grimacing, "I know you'll be able to take it. So don't get scared. You and I, Peter, are kind of outside things; not quite involved."

Caxton whispered, "Get to the point. What's up?"

Blake rose to his feet.

"Peter, the Alpha suns were pretty close two weeks ago, only about six months away at our average speed of five hundred miles a second. I thought that I would see if I could tune in some of their radio stations."

He smiled wryly. "Well," he said, "they came in all over the dials, with bell-like clarity." He paused; he stared down at Caxton, and his smile was a sickly thing. "Peter," he groaned, "we're the prize fools of creation. When I told Renfrew the truth, he folded up like ice melting into water."

Once more he paused; the silence was too much for Caxton's straining nerves.

"For heaven's sake, man—" he began. And stopped. And lay there, very still. Just like that, the lightning of understanding flashed. His blood seemed to thunder through his veins. At last, weakly, he said, "You mean—"

Blake nodded. "Yeah," he said. "That's the way it is. And they've already spotted us with their super radar. A ship will be coming out to meet us as soon as I report that you've come to. I only hope," he finished gloomily, "they can do something for Jim."

Caxton was sitting in the control chair an hour later when he saw the glint in the darkness. There was a flash of bright silver that exploded into size. The next instant, an enormous spaceship had matched velocity with them, less than a mile away.

Caxton smiled a sick smile. He said to Blake, "Did they say that that ship left its hangar ten minutes ago?"

Blake nodded. "They can make the trip from Earth to Centaurus in three hours," he said.

Caxton hadn't heard that before. Something happened inside his brain. "What!" he shouted. "Why, it's taken us five hund—" He stopped; he sat there. "Three hours!" he whispered. "How *could* we have forgotten human progress?"

In the silence that followed then, Caxton watched a dark hole open in the cliff-like wall that faced them. Into this cavern Caxton directed their ship.

The rearview plate showed that the cave entrance was closing. Ahead, lights flashed on, and focused on a door. As he eased the craft to the metal floor, a face flickered onto the radio plate.

"Cassellahat!" Blake whispered to Caxton. "The only person who's talked directly to me so far."

It was a distinguished, scholarly looking head and face that peered from the plate. Cassellahat smiled, and said, "You may leave your ship, and go through the door you see."

XIV

Caxton had a sense of empty spaces around them as they climbed into the vast receptor chamber.

A silent duo, they filed through the doorway into a hallway that opened into a very large, luxurious room.

It was such a room as a king or a movie actress on set might have walked into without blinking. It was hung with gorgeous tapestries, that is, for a moment he thought they were tapestries then he saw they weren't. They were—he couldn't decide.

He had seen expensive furniture in the office and house of Renfrew. But these settees, chairs and tables glittered as if they were made of a matching design of differently colored fires. No, that was wrong; they didn't glitter at all. They—

Once more, he couldn't decide.

Caxton had no time for more detailed examination, For a man arrayed very much as they were was rising from one of the chairs. He recognized Cassellahat.

Cassellahat came forward, smiling. Then he slowed, his nose wrinkling. A moment later, he hastily shook hands with Blake and Caxton, then swiftly retreated to a chair ten feet away, and sat down rather primly.

It was an astoundingly ungracious performance, somewhat alleviated after a moment by the man motioning them to sit down. Caxton settled into a couch near Blake, wondering.

Cassellahat began, "About your friend, I must caution you. He is a schizoid type, and our psychologists will be able to effect only a temporary recovery. A permanent cure will require a longer period, and your fullest cooperation. Fall in readily with all Mr. Renfrew's plans, unless, of course, he takes a dangerous turn.

"But now"—he squirted them a smile—"permit me to welcome you to the four planets of Centaurus. It is a great moment for me, personally. From early childhood, I have been trained for the sole purpose of being your mentor and guide; and naturally I am overjoyed that the time has come when my exhaustive studies of the middle period American language and customs can be put to the practical use for which they were intended."

He didn't look overjoyed. He was wrinkling his nose in that funny way Caxton had already noticed, and there was a generally pained expression on his face. But his words had shocked Caxton.

"What do you mean," he asked, "studies in American? Was that the English language we heard on the radio?"

"Of course," was the reply. "But the language has developed to a point where—I might as well be frank—you did have difficulty in understanding any complete sentence, didn't you?"

"But we got individual words," Blake said.

"Yes."

"Good. Then it's a matter of learning the new words?"

"Well, that's true."

They sat silent, Blake chewing his lower lip. It was Blake who finally said, "What kind of places are the Centaurus planets? You said something on the radio about the population centers having reverted to the city structure again."

"I shall be happy," said Cassellahat, "to show you as

many of our great cities as you care to see. You are our guests, and two and a half million credits have been placed to your separate accounts for you to use as you see fit." He broke off. "But if you have no more questions right now . . ."

Blake and Caxton spoke practically together: "Just a minute, sir," said Caxton. "We're loaded with questions," said Blake.

The old man bowed his acceptance of the detainment, and remained seated. It was Caxton who asked the first question. "What," he said, "about prolongation of life?"

"Twenty years," was the cautious reply, "over what you now have."

It required a little checking to make sure they were discussing the same "what you now have." But Cassellahat had learned his lessons about "middle America." And he meant approximately age seventy for their time, and age ninety for his own.

It seemed an unusually small increase. At first the disappointment of it was a shock, and then it was a puzzle. There had been so many hopes back there that medical science would shortly do something big in this area.

It appeared the problem was that cells could only renew themselves a limited number of times; originally, between ten and thirteen times, approximately every six and a half to seven years. The improvement consisted of a discovery which made it possible to produce the maximum thirteen divisions in almost every person.

But it was impossible to increase that basic maximum.

The men from the past argued that their own journey of nearly five hundred years had surely broken that barrier. But apparently it was not so. Pelham's suspended animation drug simply provided an enormous slowing down of the cellular processes, an explanation which also applied to people who lived a hundred or more years under normal circumstances.

Though Blake had interspersed a question here and there during the disappointing discussion of life prolongation, now he held up his hand. He smiled. He said, "Peter, you've been asking Renfrew's questions. Now I'll ask your questions."

He turned to Cassellahat, still smiling. "Mr. Caxton is our physicist, and I'm sure that he will be as intrested as I in what I am about to ask you."

"Please stand back a little," said Cassellahat, "while you ask." He apologized as both men drew away. "I'll explain in a few moments. But now, *your* questions, Mr. Blake."

"What," Blake began, "makes the speed of light constant?"

Cassellahat did not even blink. "Velocity equals the cube of the cube root of gd," he said, "d being the depth of the space-time continuum, g the total toleration or gravity, as you would say, of all the matter in that continuum."

"How are planets formed?"

"A sun must balance itself in the space that it is in. It throws out matter as a sea vessel does anchors. That's a very rough description. I could give it to you in a mathematical formula, but I'd have to write it down. After all, I'm not a scientist. These are merely facts I've known from childhood, or so it seems."

Caxton interrupted, puzzled. "A sun throws this matter out without any pressure other than its . . . desire . . . to balance itself?"

Cassellahat stared at him. "Of course not. The pressure involved is very potent, I assure you. Without such a balance, the sun would fall out of this space. Only a few bachelor suns have learned to maintain stability without planets."

"A few what?" echoed Blake.

Caxton could see that Blake had been jarred into forgetting the questions he had been intending to ask. Cassellahat's words cut across that thought, as he said, "A bachelor sun is a very old, cooled Class M star. The hottest one known has a temperature of one hundred and ninety degrees F., the coldest forty-eight. Literally, a bachelor is a rogue, crotchety with age. Its main feature is that it permits no matter, no planets, not even gases in its vicinity."

Blake stood silent, frowning, thoughtful. Caxton seized the opportunity to carry on a train of ideas. "Your knowing all of this stuff without being a scientist interests me. For instance, back home, by 1979 every kid understood the rocket principle practically from the day he was born. Boys of eight and ten rode around in specially made toys, took them apart and put them together again. They *thought* rocketry, and any new development in the field was just pie for them to absorb.

"Now, here's what I'd like to know: what is the parallel here to that particular angle?"

"The adeledicnander force," said Cassellahat. "I've already tried to explain it to Mr. Blake, when we were talking via the radio, but his mind seems to balk at some of the most simple aspects."

Blake aroused himself, grimaced. "He tried to tell me that electrons think; and I won't swallow it."

Cassellahat shook his head. "Not think; they don't think. But they have a psychology."

"Electronic psychology!" Caxton said.

121

"Simply adeledicnander," Cassellahat replied. "Any child—"

Blake groaned. "I know. Any child of six could tell me."

He turned to Caxton. "That's why I lined up a lot of questions. I figured that if we got a good intermediate grounding, we might be able to slip into this adeledicnander stuff the way their kids do."

He faced Cassellahat again. But the older man held up his hand. "No more, Mr. Blake. Future scientific questions should be addressed to authorities in each field, who, I assure you, are eager to meet you."

Caxton said, curiously, "All right, no more scientific questions. But what are the people like now?" He enlarged on his thought: "When we left, we were at the tail end of a fifteen-year young peoples' rebellion against the establishment—I say tail end, not because it was over, but it seemed to have leveled off about then. Stabilizing the wins or something. Whatever became of that?"

"I'm afraid," said Cassellahat reluctantly, "that I was never quite able to clarify in my own mind what that was all about—but you'll be meeting people. Tomorrow, among other things, you will be on television. You can make up your own minds."

He stood up. "Before I depart," he said, "I must give you a warning. There has been an unexpected, uh, development. At the moment that we met, I was struck by an unpleasant odor emanating from you both. At least, it's first impact on me was unpleasant, though now I am not so sure. But the problem involved needs to be studied. Until then you must be careful about close contact with human beings in this era. And this is definitely a relevant subject, for we landed several minutes ago.

"And now," he finished, "for the time being, I shall leave you. You will spend this first night still on your ship while other arrangements are made. I hope you won't mind if I wear a mask in the future in your presence. I wish you well, gentlemen, and—"

He paused, glanced past Blake and Caxton, and said, "Ah, here is your friend."

"Hi, there, fellows," Renfrew said cheerfully from the door, then wryly: "Have we ever been a bunch of suckers!"

Afterward, Caxton had a shamefaced explanation to himself for what happened then. The trip had been too much, he told himself: *For God's sake, I'm not made of steel. . . . And besides, the sudden return to sanity of someone who minutes before had been a raving lunatic —who wouldn't be slightly unbalanced by that?*

Whatever the reason that impelled him forward, *he* was the one that got to Renfrew first. He was the one who flung his arms around the man, and with tear-filled eyes hugged him.

Presently, he realized what he was doing; and he drew back, and, in a belated attempt to twist what he had done, said, "And now I'm going to punch that fellow in the jaw for what he said."

But when he turned, Cassellahat was gone.

Lying on his cot that night, Caxton couldn't sleep. At first, he told himself it was the excitement. . . . But suddenly he realized what was bothering him.

I've been conned into a wrong thought. The truth is, what does it matter who got to Centaurus first? Renfrew has it all mixed up. This is not what our goal was—to be here before anyone else from Earth. . . . Specifically, Renfrew and he—Blake's reason for coming was still unknown to Caxton—had set out for the future to locate their separate brands of immortality *for themselves*. What other men achieved meanwhile was fine—for them. What mankind accomplished during a period of five hundred years was great. But what good was that accomplishment to all the people who were in their graves?

Caxton sat up on his hard bed, intending to rush forth and point out these logical truths to Renfrew and Blake. Quickly he lay back again. He had never, he realized, so much as hinted to the others his real motives for the journey. Ridiculous to reveal a clue at this late stage. Better—as he always had—to keep his thoughts to himself.

His problem was still the same as it had been when he was in the Palace of Immortality. Presumably, all these billions of people now would also eventually be saved by the Possessors, in the sense that they would be picked up at age fourteen, or somewhere, and projected into a longer life in another probability world.

As he had then, Caxton rejected that solution irritably as meaningless. With that decision, and analysis, he was able to sleep.

XV

Caxton awakened the next morning, and for a few moments, had the thought that he was still on the trip.

Instantly he felt confused, for he couldn't remember which return to consciousness this was. The next moment awareness came, memory came.

His relief was brief. He got up. He put on his clothes—slowly.

Standing there, he realized that what he saw ahead of him was a search for the Possessors that would be greatly handicapped by his present circumstances. The three of them would probably have to remain for a time in Centaurus, and when they got back to Earth, there would be more difficulties. . . . He suddenly remembered something his first wife had said to him: "For heaven's sake, Peter, relax. Here we are making love, and I have the impression that you've already gone ahead mentally to some other experience, and that what you're doing now doesn't mean anything." It was true. He had been off in the distances of his mind, planning, scheming, nervously. Unquestionably, that kind of behavior in his past had contributed to her swift divorce suit.

Somebody had once told Caxton that a woman would never let a husband go, short of his bludgeoning her away from him. But it was not true, Caxton realized. There were some men who a woman would presently flee from, and be glad to go. He smiled his pale smile, as it occurred to him that not every man could make the statement that he was the type that a woman presently fought to get away from.

He quipped to himself: *At least I've got that going for me. I can get out of messes that I get myself into because people are glad to see me depart. Maybe I can work the same thing here.*

With that possibility, he was abruptly more cheerful. Whereupon he opened the door and stepped out into the narrow corridor, and so into the control room. He found Blake and Renfrew already there.

Blake saw him first. "I was just going to come and get you," he greeted Caxton. "We have a big medical checkup to go through, so get ready for a dull day."

Caxton said, "Oh!"

Perversely, after his long negative discussion with himself, Caxton realized that he was interested. "Maybe we can find a quick cure for the way we smell, and become attractive to women again."

The other two men brightened at those words; and so it was an interested trio that gingerly made their way out into the mental storeroom where their ship had landed, and so through a door into the same room where they had first met Cassellahat.

Cassellahat and several other persons, both men and women, were waiting for them, and stood up as they entered.

There was something about the way these people moved, a slowness, as if they had all the time in the world for what was now about to happen, that affected Caxton.

Just like that, seeing them, sensing their thoroughness, Caxton's curiosity faded.

Here was another dull thud, it seemed to him.

There were a few interesting things, however. Several machines had been brought into the room since the previous night. Cassellahat sat beside one of these and acted as an interpreter, and what he said were simple variations of "Mr. Renfrew, they would like you to take off your clothes and lie down on that table." And later: "Now, you, Mr. Blake." Finally, "Mr. Caxton—your turn."

Although he had watched the others silently undress, when it came his turn Caxton was slightly embarrassed. He was not, Caxton decided, a man who approved of women doctors. The discovery rather amazed him, for from approximately age seventeen he had maintained a ceaseless vigil for available females; constantly seeking from likely prospects intimate personal relations which —it had always been his hope—would sooner or later include total disrobement and a skin-to-skin embrace. That had never embarrassed him. So why should this?

But it did. He lay there uneasily, and watched unhappily as approximately a pint of his blood was removed. (The blood was handed out through a door, and taken off somewhere, presumably for lab tests). One of the women doctors looked into his eyes through a lens arrangement, focusing a thin beam of light into the pupil. Every twenty or so seconds, she changed the color of the light, white to red to green, yellow, and so on. Finally, she seemed to have gained the information she wanted; she went to one of the machines, where a man questioned her closely in what was evidently a debriefing interchange.

Another woman repeatedly inserted a needle into his arm or leg, or body, and squeezed one or another kind of discolored fluid into him each time. Surprisingly, he did not feel the needle pricks, which interested him, but he still cringed in anticipation at each injection thinking that this time it would be painful. The woman seemed not to notice. She was watching a series of dials, and presently she also went off to be debriefed by the man at the machine.

It was a sort of instant information approach; and it had its own appeal for Caxton. These experts were not being given time to forget what they had observed. He was about to ask a question about it when he had a thought of his own which was not just a reaction. He spoke promptly to Cassellahat.

"Be sure," said Caxton, "to inject us with the chemicals that will prolong our life expectancy to age ninety."

Cassellahat nodded gravely, but when he turned to his colleagues of the twenty-fifth century, he was smiling. And he continued to smile faintly as he "translated," if that was the right word, the instruction. It seemed to require a few moments for the others to comprehend his meaning. But suddenly they also were smiling, and several of them said something which Caxton almost, but not quite, understood.

Cassellahat turned to the three men and explained that the injections would indeed be given. But for them not to be anxious, as there were other things that came first. He continued, with a smile, "Your question, Mr. Caxton, struck one of our psychiatrists as having the implication that you felt yourself to be a visitor in a strange country who would be able to buy the local products only during the period of a short stay. Please be assured that you are now permanent residents of our era —unless you decide to take another journey using the Pelham drug; and there are reasons, which will be explained to you, why that is not a good idea."

A large, gleaming machine with an opening at one end was wheeled in, and once again the cycle ran its course: first Renfrew laid himself down in the movable, coffin-like container to which he was directed. As soon as his body was in a horizontal position, the container was rolled out of sight through the opening. He disappeared into the machine, except that his toes were visible, and at irregular intervals they wiggled.

When the container was finally wheeled out of the machine, he sat up in it, breathed hard several times, and then said, "I'll be damned!" Blake was next to go in, and finally Caxton, who lay back, thinking: *Well, they're not going to get any alarm reaction out of me.*

His first surprise came when he discovered that as his head went through the opening, and into the machine, he could see *through* the material. From where he had been watching—outside—it had looked metallically opaque. But from inside, he could see, not clearly, but as through slightly tinted glass. The faces of several of the doctors—two women and three men—pressed into convex shaped formations in the metal, as if from those peepholes *they* were watching him.

Caxton waited tensely, not knowing what to expect. Suddenly, he felt a sensation deep in his brain. Simultaneously, the little finger of his left hand twitched. Almost immediately, there was another sensation in his head. The fourth finger automatically closed upon the palm.

He lay there, then, as his fingers, then his hands, then his elbows, then his arms at the shoulders, then his toes and feet and portions of his body, were twitched. Each time, the twitch was accompanied—perhaps ever so momentarily preceded—by that odd sensation inside his head. It was a testing of reflexes on a level, and by a method undreamed of in the twentieth century.

Everything seemed to go along fine until they came

to his eyes. Caxton could feel the eye muscles twitching, and a small series of painful aches as the process continued.

Somewhere in there, the doctors withdrew over to the machine for a brief discussion; and Caxton had time to remember that, though he had never worn glasses, on occasion his vision had blurred; and he was subject to infrequent but severe eye-strain headaches. . . . He analyzed, wonderingly, that they had spotted this condition.

Shortly after he had had that thought, the medical discussion ended, and the doctors trooped back and peered in at him again. Abruptly, he experienced a sensation in his eyes that he had never had before; it was a high-speed eye-movement that he could feel as an exceedingly fast flickering motion.

"Hey!" said Caxton out loud, "what—?"

The accelerated eye motion stopped. A pause. Then the original eye muscle twitching process was repeated. This time, there was no buildup of an ache.

A minute or so after that, a breathless and admiring Caxton was wheeled out of the machine. He grew aware that a conversation was going on between the doctors and Cassellahat. The latter turned to Caxton as he got up and walked back to the chair where his clothes were.

Cassellahat said, "They want to know, where are you going, Mr. Caxton?"

He spoke gravely, and Caxton was about to take the question seriously when he realized that there was a twinkle in the older man's eyes. He did a double-take on that, took a deep breath, and said, "Am I that nervous?"

Cassellahat nodded. "Nervous, jittery, unable to lie still. You need a rest."

"I've been resting for five hundred years," said Caxton.

"They don't want to give you any tranquilizing drugs," said Cassellahat, "so try to relax. Think peaceful thoughts."

I know, thought Caxton. *The journey is over, we are here, we've got all the time we need . . . up to age ninety.* Even as he reassured himself, he realized that he didn't believe it. His attention was already leaping ahead to the moment when he could make his first move to find the trail, *in this time,* of the Possessors.

It was, of course, completely mad, he told himself. He sat there for a moment by himself, and looked around that delightful room. . . . *I ought to feel happy just to be in a place like this, having this terrific experience.*

But he wasn't happy. He watched absently as the doctors again did something with Renfrew. It occurred to him that one of the women doctors was rather good-looking. Maybe—the possibility buoyed him for a few instants of time—a female doctor would have a clinical attitude toward the odors of a male from the past, and might for strictly clinical purposes also be interested in a little sex with such a smelly type. Perhaps he ought to convey to her his own willingness to participate in such an experiment.

He was still idly having thoughts like that when Renfrew climbed to his feet and rejoined his two companions from the twentieth century. Simultaneously, all nine of the doctors filed out through a door, and disappeared.

Cassellahat came over. "They're off for lunch," he said. "Let me show you how to operate the kitchen of this apartment."

Caxton asked, "They'll be back?"

"Oh, yes; the examination is only about half over."

Later, when the examination was finally complete for all of them, one of the men doctors sat beside the debriefing machine and spoke at such length that Cassellahat at last held up his hand and stopped him. Then he turned and smiled at his charges. "He was overwhelming us with information. But, in effect, here is what he said—"

All three were in good physical health, and essentially this was also true of their mental condition. Presumably, as they became more acclimatized to their new environment—in brief, settled down—Mr. Caxton's sense of insecurity, Mr. Renfrew's feelings of loss—so that's how they were wording what had bothered Renfrew!—and Mr. Blake's uneasiness over their body odor, would be resolved by experience.

Insofar as the odor was concerned—Cassellahat spread his hands expressively as he explained, "Dr. Manadann says that smell is a volatile substance emitted by body, plant or object, and what you gentlemen emit does not seem to have these characteristics. Further tests are in order, but in a properly equipped laboratory."

There was more, but that was the essence. Several of the other doctors also spoke, but more briefly, and all that seemed to add up to the picture that apparently they carried nothing which would be infectious for the protected populations of this period of history.

This was followed by an even shorter discussion about making clothes for them that would be interwoven with and fitted with a balancing energy field. Thus, except for their heads and hands, the odor they produced could be minimized for all practical purposes. But they shouldn't go in swimming, nor strip for sun-bathing around other people.

Once again Cassellahat spread his hands and, again

smiling, said, "Well, that's it. You're free to go where you wish. The universe of 2476 A.D. is—what is the saying? —your oyster. Off you go—by tomorrow at the latest— for a good time."

Blake said, "We'd better not go anywhere except maybe on some private tours until we get those clothes."

One of the doctors spoke again, a request of some kind, as far as Caxton could make out (the language was becoming slightly less difficult-sounding). When the message was completed, Cassellahat explained that the doctors would like "one of the three gentlemen" to accompany them for additional testing. It seemed that they would prefer that it be Renfrew.

Renfrew said, "You mean, like, I'll be taken with them right now, while my two buddies"—he put his arm affectionately around Caxton, who happened to be standing close to him—"remain here?"

The sudden act of friendliness confused Caxton. *Buddies,* he thought scornfully, *that's all I need.* By the time his attention could unfix from these feelings, the arrangements were made. Renfrew and the doctors departed. Men came and wheeled away the machines. Cassellahat was the last to leave, and he paused at the door. "Well, Mr. Caxton, have you had time to form an opinion about the people of this era?"

Caxton had to admit, no. It had seemed like a pretty blank day to him, people-wise. Which was not surprising. Doctors doing their professional thing were singularly like robots, and not really like human beings.

Aloud, he said, "I thought we were going to be interviewed today, and then I'd be able to make up my mind. What about that?"

A strange look came into Cassellahat's face; he was suddenly flustered. "But"—he almost breathed the words

133

—"didn't you understand? That entire medical examination was being broadcast to all four planets." He began to recover at that point, and he apologized, "I see now that I just took it for granted that you would recognize ordinary television equipment."

"Television!" moaned Blake, who was standing off to one side.

"You mean," said Caxton, "we were being seen all day without—" He wanted to say "without any clothes on." But the words wouldn't come. His thoughts were piling up in his head, thick and fast now.

He was vaguely aware of Cassellahat speaking again. "Oh, yes. All day. You must realize, gentlemen"—he was completely calm once more—"that your arrival is a long-awaited event, and the people of all four planets are intensely interested in every detail of your stay here."

Caxton parted his lips to protest the imposition. But out of the corner of one eye he saw that Blake was trying to attract his attention. Having done so, Blake winked. And Caxton, silenced by the interruption, realized that Cassellahat was not capable of grasping what was bothering them.

Afterward, after Cassellahat was gone, and they were discussing the day and the startling revelation at its end, Caxton learned from Blake that Renfrew would be away overnight, a piece of information which he had missed during his confusion over Renfrew's gesture of affection. *Pretty slick,* he thought admiringly, *the way they whisked him off.*

Aloud, he said, "I imagine he's to be the subject of additional treatments under the guise of testing."

Blake nodded.

Caxton persisted. "Jim was unsuspicious?"

"Completely, as far as I could observe," said his companion. "In fact, he was delighted. He will be flown across the city, a privilege we won't have until tomorrow."

"I thought we were free," said Caxton, "and that we had the keys to the city."

Blake laughed. He had been allowing his moustache to grow again, and there was now a black line across his upper lip. Something of the original modern look that he had had when Caxton first met him was returning with the moustache.

He said, "Not till tomorrow, apparently. But we can remain here."

"Oh!" Caxton looked around. "In this apartment?" As Blake nodded again, Caxton said, "Well, that's at least one step forward. What time is it?"

Simultaneously, both men looked at their watches, and both were startled to realize that it was after nine in the evening. As they considered what they should do, a bell sounded softly from the kitchen. They arrived in time to see the stove mechanism (which Cassellahat had demonstrated to them at lunch) push plates loaded with steaming hot food out onto a table.

Blake ventured the guess that the food was for them, and suggested that before anyone came in to argue with that assumption, they eat.

Which they did.

On retiring to one of the bedrooms, Caxton discovered a number of pamphlets titled: *Printed Historical Guides for our Distinguished Visitors from the Past.* They were in English, and there were enough of them so that he was able to read until he fell asleep.

And that was the first full day in Alpha Centauri.

When Caxton awakened the following morning, he

was still weary from his long night of avid reading. But Renfrew was back. And so, presently, dressed and with breakfast in their stomachs, they were ready for their second day on a Centaurus planet.

XVI

THEY WERE now led out of the apartment.

It was interesting, to Caxton, to watch Renfrew; the man had already been out, and visibly felt good about pointing out to Blake and Caxton things that he had already learned.

First, they went through a door and found themselves in a gleaming corridor of the big spaceship that had come to meet them two days ago. Down some steps, then, to a floor that moved—and speeded up as soon as they got on it. When they stepped off that, they walked a short distance to another door.

As that door opened, a soft breeze met them, and they found themselves at a height but outdoors and looking over a vast gleaming concourse—some equivalent of an air field. Above was bluish-green sky, not too different from Earth's.

Except that there were two suns in the sky: one about the size of Sol was a quarter of the way up in the eastern sky. The other was bright, white, and as large as a tennis ball. It was inches away from sinking over a mountain in the west.

Caxton stopped and gazed at the scene. And for a moment, then, he forgot his own channeled purposes; and he stared, and tears came to his eyes, and he thought: *We're here! We really are!*

Beside him, Blake was saying to Renfrew, "They took you this way last night?"

"Yep."

"Lucky dog."

Renfrew said modestly that he didn't think their hosts worried about which one of them saw it all first, since they were not planning to withhold it from any of them. But he glanced knowledgeably at Cassellahat. "Same escalator?" he asked.

The old man nodded and so it was Renfrew who led the way through an opaque turnstile, and there, slanting down alongside the ship all the way to the concourse below, was a gangplank with an escalator.

A quite ordinary looking bus was waiting for them at the bottom of the escalator, and when they got inside and sat down, they were driven to a distant gate, and then onto a street that didn't look too much different from that of any large foreign city on Earth, except that the street was very wide. And what was also different was that they now saw Fly-O's for the first time.

They were driven along streets that were, every one, extremely wide, to a hotel which they entered by a back door. Then up an elevator to the very top and into a lavish penthouse apartment.

Inside, a smiling Cassellahat said, "Gentlemen from the twentieth century, among many other things yesterday, you were photographed, as a result, several suits of special clothing have been woven to measure for each of you. Your names are printed in the pockets."

He waved his hand expansively. "So find your bedrooms, get dressed, and I'll be back here when your personal Fly-O's arrive."

The Fly-O's were delivered late that afternoon. It turned out that they would not learn how they worked yet. The explaining physicist, it seemed, would come around in the late evening. But Cassellahat, who had his own machine available in the hotel checkroom for such devices, would be happy, he said, to show them the simple operational details. The three men were willing, so he took them to a large patio behind the hotel. And, slipping on his own unit, he rose vertically to a height of twenty feet and called out to his charges, "Come on!"

They came one by one, first Ned Blake, who said, "Hey!" gleefully as he soared up; then Renfrew, who went up silent but smiling; and finally, reluctantly, Caxton. His reluctance came from the fact that he swiftly observed several outward differences in this machine from the one that he had studied in the Arlay film. The earlier version had shoulder straps with a couple of loops that curled down between the legs, as an additional support. In this one, you fastened a support between the legs, which was only connected to the shoulder straps by a thin cord; and in addition you slipped two elastic mesh slipper-like things over each of your shoes. And these, also, were attached to the shoulders only by the same type of thin cord. It seemed to Caxton that there was no way in which all the separate items could work together to hold him up, since they were not bracing each other. He could see from the way the other men were holding themselves that there was some kind of interaction, but *how* they got it was not clear.

Caxton hesitated, thinking that he liked to know about such things before he trusted himself to them. Then he hesitated again, thinking that after all Blake and Renfrew really had nothing to lose because they weren't going anywhere else, and he was; *his* goal was immortality. And then he hesitated once more, thinking that it was too fast; one shouldn't have to do things like this except by gradational scale, first five feet, then ten, and maybe no higher than that the first day.

As he came to that point, he realized he was now a marked man. Blake came swooping down, and said in a low voice, "Peter, for God's sake, don't disgrace us." Caxton resisted for only a few seconds after that. Abruptly, he grabbed and gently squeezed the tiny control that hung down from one wrist.

The shoulder straps tightened first. Then there was a pressure around his seat and between his legs. And at the same time his feet grew firm. Caxton was so intent on these sensations that he was actually several feet off the ground while he was still bracing himself for the first lift. He gasped. Then he held his breath. And then he was up twenty feet with the others; and it was that simple, and it was delightful, and oh, my God!

As the four of them climbed to a height of what was eventually about five hundred feet, Cassellahat explained that that was the upper limit for individual Fly-O flight.

"But there's no real restriction," he added. "Wherever you are, over a mountain or over a sea, the machine will fly at any height up to the maximum of five hundred feet."

Caxton had not considered it a restriction. What did bother him was the conversation he overheard as he flew silent beside the other three men . . . about the journeys that were being planned, the places they would go. It had the sound of a busy itinerary, and a long time before they'd ever get to Earth. The thought saddened him, but there was nothing he could do about it.

That first flight took them over the large city of Newmerica on the planet, then out and over a bay from which a distant ocean was visible, and finally back to their hotel.

After dinner in their apartment, Caxton brought out his Fly-O unit, and, with Blake and Renfrew watching him with interest, tried to take it apart.

He couldn't even open the unit. He was still struggling with it when Cassellahat arrived with not one but two physicists and a mechanic. The difference between the 2083 A.D. Fly-O and the present one was explained to him then, while the mechanic expertly took his unit apart.

The original Fly-O operated on a compact battery which set up opposing fields around a column of what was called junk. The junk was a unit of interacting circuits which had a preset relation to the earth below. By shifting the field, the relation could be altered. Thus the Fly-O raised or lowered in order to maintain its current distance above the ground. If the junk was large enough, when the preset distance was adjusted for a greater gap, it would lift a man.

All this, it was explained to Caxton, was much too involved a process. Adeledicnander simplified the method by—what? Caxton couldn't quite get it clear. Apparently, the opposing fields were not needed because the adeledicnander electrons "knew" how to be at different heights.

Though he could not understand the science, they all three presently understood the practical operation.

And that was the second day.

On day three, they were taken up in a ship to the top of the atmosphere.

From that height, the three men from a distant time looked down on the planet. It was a tour, and a bird's-eye view of a world about the size of Earth, it said in the guidebook they each held. This one was named Blake; and after a while it was too much to see quickly.

Cities and more cities. Endless miles of agriculture, then a vast ocean. Their vessel moved through the outer fringes of the atmosphere at a speed that devoured the miles and girdled the planet in approximately seven hours. At that height and that speed it was difficult to distinguish Blake from Earth. The continents were not clearly defined; so they could have been anything, anywhere.

Each morning, Caxton got out of his beautiful bed in his fine, large room, and he looked around him, and shrugged impatiently. And, when the schedule for the day was presently announced—always somebody else's idea, never his—there was the same sense of enforcement, and the belief that ahead was another joyless day. And it was.

On their tours, he saw almost nothing. His mind was elsewhere than on the scene around, or below, or beyond. Afterwards, when Renfrew and Blake were discussing the day's activities, a dim memory would flit through Caxton's mind of the event described. And for a few moments he would smile and nod, and even make an occasional retrospective comment of his own. Sometimes—not too often—in those after-memories, he found himself tolerantly interested in the day. At such moments, he was again amazed and disappointed in himself. Because, really, he told himself, there was no hurry. Past time waits forever . . . somewhere. And yet, by the next morning, some part of him didn't believe that anymore; and there was the anger, and the frustration, and another endless day of tagging along with his two excited companions.

The change came on the eleventh day. It was noon. Blake and Caxton were in their hotel apartment. Renfrew, who had gone downstairs for an unstated reason, came in grinning. He said, "I've been hearing those low-key thoughts of yours, Peter, so I finally let them penetrate."

He explained: "You may be interested to know that I've just bought tickets to Earth for all of us, and I understand there will be some equivalent of a ticker-tape welcome awaiting us when we get there."

Silent but reflective, Caxton continued to lie on the couch, but he shook his head ever so slightly. Getting to Earth was apparently going to be as simple as Renfrew wanting it to happen.

I, he thought, feeling baffled, *couldn't have done it under three weeks or a month.*

Thinking that, he had one of his few wonders about himself, but the negative feeling didn't last very long. Because . . .

To Earth. Thank God.

XVII

THEY MADE the trip, of course, in three hours; and of course, it took almost as long to get to their hotel from the spaceport through the cheering crowds.

That night—when asked by interviewers on an around-the-world broadcast—what he wanted most to see on Earth, Caxton said, "The city of Lakeside."

The interviewers were astonished. "But why? You were not born there. That isn't where you lived."

"I dreamed it," said Caxton blandly. He embellished his lie. "Somewhere in the long sleep, perhaps as I was coming to, that name came to me, and so I'm curious. Obviously"—with the same blandness—"after five centuries, we can only look at our home towns like people exploring archaeological remains. Naturally, I want to go there. But Lakeside first."

It was a bold thought, it seemed to him, to name the city where he had emerged from the Palace of Immortality—several hundred years ago. But he had to believe that the Possessors *knew* that it was he who had gone along on this incredible journey, and they must know, also, that he had a purpose connected with them. So his presence here was not a secret.

No, no, thought Caxton, *they can see me, but I can't see them.* His hope was that his frankness and his sincerity—as proved by his coming this tremendous distance in time—would now win him the entry that had earlier (somewhere) been denied him.

That, it seemed to him, was his simplest and most direct possibility.

The camera crew had come directly to the hotel; and so, as Caxton emerged from his part of the interview, Blake was waiting for him at the door. Through the transparencies behind Blake, Caxton could see that several other men were watching him as if they had personal plans for him.

But it was Blake first, and Blake who said, "That's the one that does it, Bud." Caxton had an idea of what was coming, and braced himself. He considered Blake a formidable individual, and it had simply been his good luck so far that the man's attention had been on his former boss. Thus he had avoided a direct confrontation with one of the shrewdest people he had ever met—until now.

Blake continued, "Peter," he said, and he shook that dark-haired head of his chastisingly, "you never lived in Lakeside, did you?"

Caxton had to admit, no, he hadn't.

"In fact, if I recall correctly, your home city is about five hundred miles further west." When Caxton said nothing, Blake asked, "Have you ever been to Lakeside?"

Caxton decided that his one trip there in the year 2083 A.D. didn't count as a visit. So he shook his head once more, and tried this time to put on a somewhat mystified expression.

"Okay, okay!" Blake was shaking his head. "If that's the way you want it, my friend, that's the way it will be." He caught Caxton's arm in a comradely gesture, and drew him through the door to the men who were waiting outside the broadcast room. "There's a man here who wants to meet you." He beckoned and a stern-faced man

145

in his forties came forward. Blake said, "Mr. Bustaman, I want you to meet my friend, Peter Caxton. Peter, this is—" He said a word that sounded like "Schlemiel," but of course that was impossible, and after such a beginning Caxton dared not ask for the name again. Something Bustaman. He left it at that; and was murmuring his acknowledgment when for the first time he actually looked at the man.

It was a moment of *deja-vu*. Not, "I've been here before," but "I've seen this man before." *Where?* Caxton began to tremble. In the twentieth century—where else? And if that was so, then . . . then—

Blake was speaking again. "Mr. Bustaman differs from most of the people we have met in this era because like Cassellahat he speaks Middle American just about like a native."

A Possessor!

What saved Caxton from standing there and giving himself away, for he was actually overwhelmed, was that the other men were pressing forward, smiling, shaking his hand, murmuring words in the dialect of the time which Caxton could now understand, somewhat, and to which he responded in his slow way of speaking each word.

And with each passing moment, he was recovering his front, which was normally made of marble and iron; and every instant he was thinking, *Where? Who?* During that minute and a half of rapid introductions, his memory ranged over his entire experience with the Possessors and it was not so much, then, that he was able to visualize Bustaman aged to seventy years, but that in wildly casting his thought over the various people he had seen in, and in connection with, the Palace of Immortality, his mind focused swiftly on one person.

That old man. . . . What was it the salesman, Kellie, had said: "He looks like all the tough sales managers in the world"?

I've got to keep contact with this fellow! As they were separating, he said as much in his desperation—and got a surprised look from Bustaman. "But, of course," said the man, politely, "I'll see you in the morning, as we have just arranged."

"For God's sake, Peter"—it was Blake—"you've done it again." He caught Caxton around the shoulders with one arm, laughed in a friendly but slightly apologetic fashion, and, leaning forward, explained to Bustaman, "We can't seem to get this man all the way into the twenty-fifth century. He keeps slipping . . . somewhere." To Caxton, Blake said, "Mr. Bustaman has a private air yacht that everyone agrees is superior in comfort to what the government has available; so he will be taking us to Lakeside tomorrow."

XVIII

THE PROCESSION of machines that flew along to Lakeside the next day consisted of Bustaman's beautiful ship, a government protective vessel, and a large craft with camera crews and reporters, who, apparently, would be following their every move.

The interior of Bustaman's luxury ship was the size of a private railroad car; and, except that it was streamlined in the familiar airstream style, that was just about the way it looked from the outside, also. Caxton sat in a plush chair beside a huge view window; what bothered him was that, presumably, he had already achieved his purpose. The sudden appearance of Bustaman was, in its way, all that he had hoped to accomplish in mentioning Lakeside at all.

Nonetheless, he decided he would not waste the trip, but would boldly try to locate the house he wanted. . . .

There was only one trouble, it developed, with that goal. When the expedition reached Lakeside, and under his guidance flew back and forth over the city, he couldn't find anything that looked like the house.

He kept telling himself that hills were essentially changeless. Hard to believe that someone—a builder, a city planning commission, a military necessity, or whatever—had taken the time, the trouble, and the money to level a viewsite like the one on which *the* house had stood in 2083 A.D.

Yet, in all Lakeside, there were visible only two major hill formations. Caxton approached them from all angles—and only succeeded in confusing himself. From the air and from the ground there was nothing that resembled what he had seen. Of course, it was now four hundred years later. On one of the hilltops, the city had constructed a museum, which was rather stupid, it seemed to a highly irritated Caxton. When, on checking, he learned that it had been built only forty-eight years before, he began to have the sickening suspicion that this was indeed the spot; and that here, as a result of somebody's idiocy, was the end of his hope.

They flew back to New York late in the afternoon. Caxton had the feeling that he must look like a fool to those people who had watched him on their wall screens all day—or at least on and off all day. He couldn't accept that anybody was still that interested in the visitors from the past so that they would continue to put their principal attention on such a dull event as a journey in search of nothing.

Yet, when he was questioned on television that night, the interviewers seemed to be intent, seemed to take him seriously, and were enormously interested in his statement that perhaps what he was looking for could not be found in a one-day visit. He therefore stated it as his intention to move to Lakeside for a while.

"But what do you expect to find, Mr. Caxton?" the interviewer insisted.

"I don't know. I have a feeling I'll know it when I see it."

The man was smiling. "Mr. Caxton, you have certainly captured the imagination of this rather prosaic era with that mystic dream of yours. It has some of the aspects of the ancient quest for the Holy Grail, and we shall"—he looked up at the camera—"keep our viewers informed of the progress of the quest. Good luck, sir."

He held out his hand, and Caxton shook it. On his way to his room, he was thinking: *My quest is for immortality, and for that quest I have the same fanaticism as those long-ago crusaders. In fact—*

It occurred to him that for what the announcer knew of his purpose, the comparison was inappropriate and even lacking in good taste. But there *was* a similarity to his real, hidden goal. For those quest-seekers long ago there had come the dreadful awareness that man was mortal; and so they had done in their way and for their time what he was doing now, with the same total commitment. Had theirs been madness? He had always thought so. Was his? If it was, or wasn't, either way it was impossible to give up. What else was there to do? Go back to Centaurus?—he couldn't care less. Get involved with the twenty-fifth century? Grudgingly, he agreed with Blake and Renfrew that such a thing was not impossible, but it wouldn't be easy. They were like immigrants from a very backward country, and such types usually settled in some ghetto of their own kind. Only there was no such ghetto for immigrants out of time.

That night, while Blake and Renfrew watched him wordlessly—for a while—Caxton packed his clothes. Aware of their eyes following his movements, he felt infinitely foolish, and yet determined. It was Caxton who finally broke the silence. "I'll be gone for a few days. I hope you don't mind."

The two men exchanged glances, and then Renfrew came over to where Caxton was bending over his suitcase, and threw one arm over his shoulder. He said impulsively, "We're going with you, pal. Ned and I can work out of Lakeside just as easily as from anywhere else. Okay?"

It was another one of those crazy, emotional moments. . . . *For God's sake,* thought Caxton as he fought back the tears, *if I don't watch out for these two one of these days I'll burst out crying like a woman, and tell them the whole mad story.*

They moved to Lakeside.

Bustaman came along. "After all," he said, "I'm independently wealthy. So I'll just place myself at your disposition. I have nothing else that I'd rather do."

Caxton considered that grimly. It was beginning to seem certain that even the "opposition" in the Palace of Immortality was not planning to make things easy for him.

XIX

DURING THE next seventeen days, Caxton's daily journal
—if he had had the patience to write one—could have
read:

> Went to Piffer's Road every day for a week. It's
> now part of Central East 42, which consists of a
> long shopping mall, running thirty-seven and a half
> miles from somewhere north of Warwick Boulevard
> to somewhere south of Kissling Drive, with a lake
> of residences extending along either side. There are
> seventy-three Central East cities of this type. This
> is what Cassellahat meant when he said that there
> had been a return to the city structure. In Central
> East 42, I found no clue to the Palace of Immortality.
> . . . It is the middle of the second week. I man-
> aged to give everybody the slip, and have hired a
> research firm to trace down the ownership of all
> the houses on the two hills in Lakeside. It will take
> a few days.
> . . . Well, it appears that a family named Magoel-
> son owned one of the houses until the property was
> taken over for the museum. And that in every gen-
> eration, the head of the Magoelson family was called
> Daniel. The research firm is now tracing down the
> Magoelson family in this generation. They expect to
> have the address(es) for me by tomorrow or the

*day after. Is this it? Have I found a Possessor of the
main Palace group? I hope so. Renfrew and Blake
are becoming restless. . . .*

That night—of the day he had that thought—Renfrew
and Blake invited him out for a drink. Caxton went, but
he was uneasy. Something in their manner . . .

In the darkness of the bar, they raised their glasses at
Blake's suggestion, and drank to the beautiful women of
all ages. Having sipped from his glass, Blake made a face,
and said, "As we may now surmise, people probably reflect in their body odors the food they eat. Thus, Chinese dogs of our time barked ferociously at white visitors, and ignored Chinese travelers, who presumably ate
the same food as the people of the village. And so it
could be that we wouldn't care to associate closely with
a woman of Shakespeare's day, and would be quite willing to leave Cleopatra to Caesar and Marc Anthony. Bath-
ing apparently is not the factor. Large quantities of
cologne help, but it looks like we may have to subject
our cells to several more months of the current era diet
before we finally merge into the universal smell."

He paused; and Caxton, who was beginning to feel relieved—the conversation so far didn't seem to be too
different, or any more significant than previous ones—
did one of his square "things," as he realized afterward:
he actually took Blake's words at their face value. He
said, "I've looked into that a little. I think it's the fer-
tilizer they used then, and now. In old China, you may
recall, human feces was carefully fed back into the soil
with nauseating results, from the Western point of view.
Here, they use a chemical compound, unknown in our
time."

He was about to give a more detailed description of

the substance, when he caught a look in Renfrew's eyes, and stopped. "What's up?" he asked.

Blake parted his lips to speak again, but Renfrew placed a restraining hand on his friend's arm, and said with his smile, "Remember when you two offered me your money. I said I had a thought—"

Caxton could feel a change in his face.

He had forgotten.

The gift of two and a half million credits from the governments of the four habitable planets of the Centaurus suns was apparently a division into three equal amounts of money that Renfrew had invested for them in government bonds five hundred years before. At the time, a law had been passed authorizing such a long-term investment, and of course it was an arbitrary government act that had now divided it equally among the surviving time travelers. All the money in truth belonged to Renfrew.

Shortly after this source of the lavish funds was clarified, Blake had immediately offered his share to Renfrew and, after the slightest hesitation, so had Caxton. To his disappointment, Renfrew had not immediately rejected the proffered money. At the time he said with a smile, "Let's leave things as they are. But I've got a thought about something that may require me to ask you both to chip in rather extensively. If that materializes, then I'll take a raincheck. Otherwise, forget it."

Which was a pretty generous statement. But it sort of left the money not Caxton's.

Now, he braced himself for disaster, thinking: *Am I going to have to make an accounting?*

Renfrew was continuing; "I'm delighted to tell you that it has worked out." He grinned at Caxton affectionately. "These last few weeks while you've been charging

around looking over this town, Ned and I have been pric-
ing super-spaceships. Well, my friend"—he put out his
hand and, with that magnetic touch, lightly grasped
Caxton's wrist—"we can get one for five and a half
million credits. So I thought—"

Renfrew had turned away from Blake in his jubilance;
and so, as Caxton looked, he caught Blake's eyes on him
from beyond Renfrew. Blake made a nodding gesture
with his head, and his eyes appealed to Caxton to go
along with the idea whatever it was.

Renfrew was finishing his proposition, "Why don't we
all put up equal sums, and jointly purchase the ship
that Ned and I have chosen?"

Caxton had been making a rapid calculation, dividing
five and a half by three; and since one third was less
than what he had by more than half a million credits,
it meant nothing; it was as unreal a sum as the original
amount, which he had never possessed anyway in his
own mind.

There was enough left for his private purposes. So
the request was a nothing to him, to be acceded to
without a single, further thought.

In fact, he had no thought—and no suspicion.

"Great!" he said loudly; too loudly. "Consider it done.
In fact—"

He drew out his checkbook and wrote a check to
James Renfrew for the entire one and five-sixths million credits. He presented it with a flourish, and realized as he did so that Blake had been telling him their
plans.

Caxton was vaguely aware of Renfrew accepting the
check. But inside him there was an awful pause. . . .
What did he say? What trip?

Blake was speaking glowingly. "Tomorrow, we'll check

out the ship. But it's automatic. No problems. Then the next day, we leave."

Caxton stared at him blankly. And then—he couldn't help himself—he said, "For God's sake, where are we going?"

Blake said with shining eyes, "Peter, this is one of the ships that can go to Centaurus in three hours, to Sirius in about ten, and so on." It was he now who reached across to Caxton, gripped his arm. His gaze sought Caxton's eyes. "Look, boy, we've gone along with your little game here. Now, you go along with Jim's for a couple of months of space exploration. Okay?"

"We'll cruise for a while," said Renfrew. "What do you say, pal?"

He didn't resist. He couldn't resist. Not yet. Strange, but he still felt bound to the other two men; could not bring himself to oppose their plans. Many times, he thought: *It's because they like me, and I haven't had that before from anyone. . . .* But there was also the factor that if—*if*—he had to stay in the twenty-fifth century, then it could be that he would need their companionship more, even, than they needed his. After all, they always had each other. In that department, he was definitely second. Blake would always put Renfrew first, and Renfrew would always, well, expect Blake to put him first. But it seemed to be true that they *both* gave some of their affection to a jittery, nervous, tense, jumpy, absentminded potential-betrayer-of-their-trust, a peculiar mixed-up individual named Peter Caxton, who had a twentieth century M.A. degree in physics and an all-across-the-board idiot's degree in yearning for immortality. And because he needed the good feeling that they offered him, he couldn't help it—he had to hold still for what they wanted. And so there was no avoiding this exploratory trip into space.

Caxton stayed in the lobby of the hotel, trying to think how he might speed up the search for the present address of Dan Magoelson. Because if he could go there . . .

What then? He realized that he visualized an entrance into the Palace of Immortality through Magoelson's home. And if it was there, he would sneak into the Palace and hide. Once inside . . . His plans were vague, but to hell with that. He'd face that situation when he got to it, but in the back of his mind he was aware of the shadowy hope that he could make a delaying agreement with the Possessors, whereby they allowed him to remain while he made the effort to fit his personality to their requirements.

Surely Caxton thought as he paced from one end of the lobby to the other, with the coffin staring him in the face as the only alternative, he could become—he laughed curtly—a softer, gentler, more appealing Peter Caxton. It was difficult to imagine such a change, but other people were like that; so why not he? Still, the problem had never really been with *him*. His own personality had taken its present form as he gradually, and rather unwillingly, became aware of the madness of other people. One out of every two gave him a hard time.

Maybe they can change me, but how in God's name are they ever going to change those millions of SOB's out there that I have to deal with? It seemed to his restless mind that his perception of the environment would have to be dimmed before he dared let down his guard.

Toward ten o'clock in the evening, his feverish excitement diminished suddenly. Caxton knew the sign. He had exhausted himself with his overstimulated thoughts. Now would come the period of apathy and resignation.

He was actually turning to go wearily up to his room when for the first time he remembered Bustaman. Instantly the excitement surged again, more tiredly, but it was enough to send him to a communicator cubbyhole, and from its silent interior to contact the man who was the enemy of the principal group of Possessors. By the time the now-familiar, remembered, stern face appeared on the plate, Caxton had his cool back and his story ready.

Which was a sort of thank-you-for-everything-hope-we-see-each-other-again-when-we-get-back-from-our-journey. Unspoken was: *Now, do something!*

What happened then was like an almost invisible hope far in the back of his mind, being brought into focus. Bustaman seemed momentarily taken aback. But he recovered swiftly and spoke the magic words. "Uh, Peter, why don't I come over in my Air Special and pick you up at the hotel, and we go somewhere for a little chat? Is that okay with you?"

It was A-okay.

Caxton rushed first to his room. Into various little pockets of his keep-the-odor-in suit, he slipped his Browning .25 automatic, a couple of extra clips of ammunition, a laser cutting device that he had picked up in a store, a tiny tube of food capsules, a gas gun from the twenty-fifth century and half a dozen stimulants designed to keep the waking center of the brain alert even though the sleep center was at "on." One of these he swallowed.

There were several other devices that, it seemed to him in a sudden onslaught of anxiety, he would like to take with him. But he fought the fear and restrained his defensive instincts. . . . He arrived on the hotel roof less than a minute before Bustaman's machine settled down on its silent adeledicnander power in one of the landing spaces.

The door of the craft opened. The ramp folded silently down. Caxton, intent and feeling accepted, was about to start up it, when he saw that Bustaman had come to the entrance, and was blocking it.

Bustaman said in a deliberate tone, "Well, Peter, the hour of reckoning has come, eh?"

Those words were quietly spoken by a man who was perfectly aware that Caxton had recognized him . . . during the moment of introduction by Blake. He wanted Caxton to be aware of that also, and to realize that what was now about to happen would have to be undertaken by decision.

Bustaman had pride. It was, perhaps, the one quality that had distinguished him from the other Possessors. Being proud, he looked at the others from a slightly-apart stance. What saved him from discovery in his own first days in the Palace was his smile. Later he would lose it, but in the beginning he always smiled as if he was with them.

He wasn't. And so it was he who observed that Claudan Johns also was a person apart. That, just as there were no probability duplicates of Kameel Bustaman, so there were none of Claudan Johns.

Johns, observing Bustaman, noticed the absence of Bustaman probabilities, but, being gentle in nature, it never occurred to him to regard the absence as a Bustaman vulnerability. But Bustaman, observing Johns, realized with a developing glee that right there was the weakness of *all* of them; that he could stop the entire probability madness by striking at one key figure.

Peter Caxton was the man he had selected to do the striking. He anticipated no problems from Caxton. Because, of course, he intended to say the magic words, "Peter this is your route into the Palace of Immortality."

He also planned to say, "I had to let these weeks go by, so that you'd realize that they weren't going to come to your rescue, and that in fact they haven't given you another thought since they kicked you out."

His additional instructions would include the requirement that Caxton must change his clothes to fit the twentieth century. "Because that's where you're going, Peter. . . ."

As he had anticipated, Caxton, when offered the choice, almost fell over himself in his eagerness to accept.

XX

Dust. He sat in the dust beside a dirt road.

Caxton looked around him with eyes that presently recognized Piffer's Road in its drab twentieth century condition. Somewhere off to his left—he caught a glimpse in the distance to the east—was little Jimmy's white house. A man's equally distant figure was walking rapidly toward the railroad farther east. . . . *Is that me, then?* Caxton wondered. He had no impulse to check. Across from where he sat was a fence, and, beyond, the wilderness of a scantily inhabited countryside.

He turned to stare up the road. He could see trees not too far away, and, partially visible through the leaves and branches, a large rust-colored trailer.

That brought him to his feet with a gasp. It had to be *this* trailer.

He began to run, past another house, past some old tin cans, a bunch of willows in the ditch, a gleam of stagnant water; and then, as he turned into the tree-lined open space where the trailer was parked, he slowed, gasping, and walked rapidly to the door of the trailer.

It was as he was entering that he remembered that Jimmy would later report this event, and that meant Jimmy was hiding somewhere nearby. Caxton didn't let it slow him down. Because, as he also recalled, in Jimmy's story he had barely gotten inside and barely hidden himself when the owners returned.

And so into the trailer he went headlong, trusting that it was all true. He stumbled back along a tiny corridor and so on into the rear storage room—and crouched as out of sight as he could manage in one corner.

Suddenly, voices. A man's and a woman's.

Hiding there, Caxton wondered what might happen even now if he should be caught red-handed before he could act. He heard the man say, "We'll head for the fourteenth century."

The male voice went on, grimly, "You'll notice that it's still just one man we have to deal with. So he has had to go out and spend thirty or forty years growing old, because old men have so much less influence on an environment than young. Didn't want to affect the twentieth century more than he already had. But now—transformer points, and go into the cab and start the motors."

It was the moment Caxton had been waiting for. He stepped out softly, flexing his gloved right hand. He saw the man standing facing in the direction of the door that led to the front room and the engine cab beyond it. From the back, the man looked of stocky build, and about forty-five years of age. In his hands, clutched tight, he held two transparent cones that glowed with a dull light.

"All right," he called gruffly, as Caxton stepped up behind him. "We're moving. And hereafter, Selanie, don't be so frightened of one guy, however vicious. The one thing I've managed to do is make sure that none of that crowd of one can ever get near us without—"

His voice collapsed into a startled grunt as Caxton grabbed his shoulder and pressed hard below the collarbone.

The stocky man stood utterly still, like a man who

has been stunned by an intolerable blow. And then, as Caxton let go of his shoulder, he turned slowly, and his gaze fastened sickishly, not on Caxton's face, but on the glove he wore.

"A Destroyer glove!" he whispered; and then more wildly, "But how? The repellers are on, my special invention that prevents a trained Possessor from coming near me!" He looked for the first time at Caxton's face. "How did you do it? I—"

"Father!" It was the girl's voice, clear and startled, from the engine cab. Her voice came nearer. "Father, we've stopped at about A.D. 1650. What's happened? I thought—"

She paused in the doorway like a startled bird, a tall, slim girl of around nineteen years, looking suddenly older, grayer, as she saw Caxton. Her gaze fluttered to her father. She gasped. "Dad, he hasn't—"

The stocky man nodded hopelessly. "Wherever we are in time and space, we're *there*. Not that that matters. The thing is, we've failed. Bustaman has won."

The girl turned toward Caxton again. "Why, you're that man—" She stopped; then: "Didn't I see you on that train just now?" Once again she stopped, shaking her head. "There were so many people, but you look familiar."

Caxton was having his own problem of orientation to her, and to the realization that to these people he was a stranger. He recognized Selanie herself, but not vividly. In fact, it was difficult to take his mind back to that journey on the train, and to what the salesman, Kellie, had told him about her. Except for the train incident and the brief personal encounter with a much older Selanie in the Palace of Immortality, that was all he remembered of the girl.

163

The sudden realization disturbed Caxton. *I've done this thing,* he thought, *to two people I don't know and who don't know me.*

He recognized now where his feeling of false familiarity had started: that statement about the older Selanie being his wife in a particular probability world had impressed her identity on his mind. All the rest he had been told by other people, and he recalled none of it, really, in terms of personal experience.

These various truths came flashingly to his attention as he stood there inside the trailer, his gaze intent on the girl and her father. Finally, he answered her question. "Yes," he said, "I followed you because this is my way into the Palace of Immortality."

The girl was staring at him. "Oh, you fool!" she whispered. "You've been tricked. You're doomed with us."

Caxton, returning her stare, felt a sinking inside him. He was remembering that Bustaman had made no statement about how he would be rescued. The old man's other reassurances seemed suddenly less meaningful, for Caxton had somehow assumed that this trailer utilized the Palace for its time travel. And that was visibly not so.

Before he could part his dry lips to say anything, the girl said, "He can't rescue you below 1977, because no one but my father knows how to go earlier than that, and you've just ruined his ability to travel in time. We're somewhere in the middle sixteen hundreds—and there's nothing in this period of time that is useful for time travel."

With each word that she spoke, Caxton's sense of disaster took another downward leap. And when she finally finished, there he was, at the bottom of his hope.

1650 A.D., about, in America. Why, that was before—

he couldn't remember the timing of it exactly, but beyond all question, no white man had penetrated at that time this far into the interior.

With that realization, his mind went blank.

XXI

CAXTON'S FIRST awareness after that came when he saw the girl turning away. There were tears in her eyes as she opened the outer door and jumped to the green grass below.

His impulse was to follow her, to apologize, to make amends, somehow. But he was not a man who had ever trusted a woman's reality. And so he hesitated, and then said to her father, "Is it true? We're stuck here?"

The older man's lean head did not face him directly. Instead, his gray eyes turned in their sockets, slightly, and studied him. "The problem," Johns said finally, "is because as the experimenter I did not participate in the experiment. Also, I requested my daughter to refrain from participating so that she might assist me in the eventual evaluation. She did go into a few probability worlds, but each time—at my request—she terminated them, and merged again into one person. Thus, whoever-you-are, I am today a guilty man. For, because of my insistence and her loyalty—and because the time foldback in which the Palace of Immortality functions operates only from 9812 A.D. back to 1977, but not to the seventeenth century—neither Selanie nor I have any place we can go. And so, yes, here we are. I can see no way out."

There were too many meanings for Caxton to grasp all the details. But the conclusion was clear. Trembling, he walked to the open door and, stepping down to the ground, ventured forth upon a green wilderness world.

He saw that the girl had climbed what in the twentieth century had been a small wooded hill. Here, the hill had no trees on it; and, though he had no clear purpose in connection with her or the situation, he strode up also, and presently was standing near her.

Remembering Indians, he glanced at the girl fleetingly only; gazed instead at the vista of land around them. He had a surprisingly hard time seeing it, for images of Piffer's Road from other times kept associatively intruding.

But a wind was blowing, that was real upon his face and not a memory. And the air was crystal-clear, except for a faint blue mist that half sheathed a distant hill. In all the miles between that hill and this one, there was not a ground movement—not an animal, not a human. A few birds were flying in the distance, but they were too far away to identify.

Clouds were up there, also, and the wind in those higher reaches must have been of spanking proportions; for the clouds moved with visible speed across the sky.

"Well," Caxton said, relieved, "we won't be having to defend ourselves today."

The girl's back was to him. Without turning, she said, "Mr. whoever-you-are, the first Indians who saw white men were friendly. So we mustn't assume threat where it may not exist."

It was true enough. Yet the remark brought Caxton mentally as well as visually all the way down from the sky. He was suspicious of the ideals of the young because there were so many that conflicted. And her remark had the particular implication of the anti-violence school that pretended that they themselves were not violent, and therefore had the right to judge human history.

Nonetheless, when he spoke it was in a neutral tone. "Still, Indians fought among themselves before the white man came. And my name is Peter Caxton."

He was watching her closely as he spoke. But if she recognized the name, it did not show in her back, her neck, or in the way she held her head.

Caxton felt baffled.

But this, he decided, was not the moment for such minor matters. He was the villain of this tragedy—that was what counted. That was what he must, somehow, counterbalance.

"Miss Selanie," he began haltingly, "I seem to have made a grave error in judgment. Not only have I committed a harmful act against you and your father, but evidently I myself was duped into believing that—"

He was cut off. "Mr. Caxton," said the woman, "I would rather you didn't apologize. When I look over the situation which you have created, I can see what a man will eventually expect from it, and I wish to make it very clear, Mr. Caxton, that your cells somehow reflect a lower-grade body condition, and therefore you and I—here—shall never have a personal relationship. Is that understood?"

It was so direct and unexpected that Caxton turned pale. Before he could recover from the impact of her words, or, more important, consider the meaning of what she had said, she turned and walked rapidly down the hill.

Watching her, a fear came that she would go inside the trailer and lock the door on him. And she and her father would drive away, leaving him here on this lonely prairie. He began to run down the slope after her. She must have heard him, for she slowed. He passed her at a dead run. And so he reached the door first. With an enormous inward effort, he controlled that sudden terror, controlled it enough so that he opened the door, and held it for her, and then, still breathing hard from the unaccustomed exercise, stepped in behind her. Safe.

He was ashamed of himself then. But that emotion merely superimposed itself on the remnants of his sudden fear. There was a stool in the middle room opposite the door and Caxton sat down on it, struggling for more control of his trembling body.

He assured himself that they didn't seem afraid of him. And that was amazing, because for all they knew he was a criminal. No fear, no anxiety, no concern that he might do them more damage. The girl seemed to accept him as a gentlemanly sort, one who could be controlled by a woman's rejection.

Caxton visualized the three of them alone here in this wild, pre-white America for thirty more years; and during that whole time, presumably, she would be an untouchable queen and he would be the unworthy peasant who had better not aspire.

An undeterminable number of minutes went by, and the seethe of emotions in him would not subside. During that time the girl came through the middle room several times. On each occasion she glanced at him and said nothing. And each time, when she was gone, he was aware of the sound of cooking utensils loud and clear within inches, it seemed, of his eardrums.

Finally the girl came out. "Dinner, Mr. Caxton," she said.

He went forward without a word. And there was the tiny table of the trailer set for three. Selanie motioned him to squeeze in at the far end. They ate silently. The father sat opposite Caxton, but stared at the wall beyond him, eating silently. The girl sat, apparently at ease as she ate. And Caxton was halfway through the meal before he realized that another set of thoughts was rushing in the usual disordered way through his mind.

First thought: *Dinner! Is it that late?* He recalled having seen the sun when he was on the hilltop with the girl, but he could not remember where in the sky it had been. From the greenness of the grass and the trees, he guessed it was middle or late spring, and a warm day; so the sun would be describing its arc virtually at the zenith. Therefore, when they were out, it should have been sinking toward the west.

Okay, he thought wearily, *so I remain the world's worst observer. I'm the guy that's always in such a dither that it doesn't really matter whether it's day or night, raining or shining. . . .* Except, he realized ruefully, he would now have plenty of time to observe such minutiae of nature.

Years, in fact decades—but a limited number of those. Because, of course—he laughed a silent, grim, deep-inside laugh—this was the end of the quest for immortality of Peter D. (for donkey) Caxton. He wondered if Bustaman had known that this trailer could go into time earlier than the Palace of Immortality time fold. It was hard to believe that because the fact was that Bustaman did need new associates. His was a pretty small group, consisting apparently of one person: himself.

Dinner ended slightly less silently than it had begun. As Selanie started to clear the dishes off into a tiny sink, Caxton came to, and asked, "May I help?"

But she refused him with a shake of her pretty

head, and a "No thank you, Mr. Caxton. Your room is at the rear of the trailer, and I would appreciate it if you would go there or outside."

Since he wasn't about to go outside, Caxton retreated to the rear room and there found that a wall cot had been folded down into the only space left in that crowded room. The door of that room, fortunately, was a sliding type, and so he quickly sealed himself in, wondering what the breathing facilities were in such a narrow space. They were perfect, and silent.

His own experience with pumped-in air was that the fan made at very least a faint hissing noise. Curious, he began a tentative search for the ventilation system, but though he could feel a movement of air through the room, it was not directional enough for its source to be located in such a small space.

Presently, he lay down on the cot, and thought of taking an after-dinner nap. But as he sprawled, hopefully waiting for sleep, he suddenly remembered they had had steak for dinner: there would be a limited amount of that; and then he would have to become the hunter and meal provider. *What happens then,* he thought, *my fair lady, to your aloofness when I am man, the provider, in a primitive world?*

That's how it all started, baby. In those (these?) days, food was hard to get, and the human females attached themselves to men who could go out there and get it. You mean to tell me you think I'll make all that effort, and not have female companionship as my just reward? If you do, you—

That was as far as he got. At that point, from the near distance—not inside the trailer—he heard a sharp, cracking sound. It took a moment, because he was not accustomed to the sound; it took a long moment before he realized what it was: *Gunshot!*

Caxton sat up, swung his legs off the cot and knocked over two boxes. Their contents tumbled around him, as he searched under the cot for his shoes. Finally he had the shoes on, unlaced. Up he stood, and stepped across the cot to the door. Forgetting it was a sliding door, he fought what he kept thinking was the latch.

Then he had the door open and he ran awkwardly, with his untied shoelaces interfering, through the next room and the outer door—which was shut. Opening it, he was relieved to see that it was still light outside, a kind of bright twilight.

Coming toward him, along what would later—much later—be Piffer's Road, was Selanie. In her left hand she carried a rifle and in her right, swinging by the legs with head hanging, was a bird about the size of a large pigeon, except that it was brownish in color. Caxton, who was extremely vague about which birds were which, nevertheless guessed that this particular specimen was a partridge or a prairie chicken, or perhaps even a type of pheasant.

As the girl came up to him, she held the creature forward for him to inspect. "I saw it come down from the sky and land near a clump of bushes," she said in a cheerful voice, "so I sneaked up on it—and we'll all have a bite or two for breakfast."

She added in the same happy voice, "I've appointed myself huntress, cook, and food provider in general. That should keep me busy."

"B-but." Caxton had seated himself on the grass and was tying his shoes. "But what do *I* do?"

The girl shrugged her slender shoulders. "Men like you tend toward philosophy," she said. "Kind of low-level, kind of endless, think-think, but still, it's in the frame. Just keep on doing it," she finished.

Having uttered the casual judgment and consigned him to a future of introspection, she walked on into the trailer. Since the door stayed open, Caxton remained where he was.

It had become darker during those few minutes, and the stars were visible in the sky in increasing numbers. As he lay back and looked up at them, a coyote howled in the distance. Caxton, who in his life had never heard a coyote, nevertheless recognized the cry from descriptions he had read. What startled him was that the animal was undoubtedly only making its sound, but to his ears, and to something in his brain, it sounded deeply mournful.

For the first time he recalled something that a friend —no. He consciously corrected the term: an acquaintance (he had no friends)—had once told him: that there were no really dangerous animals in North America. Be wary of bears, which meant, simply, turn aside and stay clear . . . and there was nothing else. Cougars did not seek men; men sought them. And the animal had such a peculiar, friendly interest in human beings that it would hold still to be murdered. Step away from rattlesnakes; don't get in the path of a rampaging herd of buffalo—and that was it. Nothing else on the entire continent was ordinarily dangerous to a human adult.

Okay, he thought in irritation, *so I was philosophizing; so I don't change her mind by being the big, successful hunter and killer.*

Back on his cot, finally, he realized he was relieved.

And that was their—his—first day in the mid-seventeenth century of what would one day be the United States.

Day two!

After breakfast, which Caxton ate silently, he went to his room since he was still unwilling to trust himself outside while they were in, and lay down on the cot to consider what he should do with his time. The minutes went by, and he couldn't think of anything. Oh, a conversation or two with Mr. Johns: how did the glove work? How had it damaged him? How come Caxton was not damaged when he was grabbed by the elbow with the same type of glove?

A few other questions occurred to him as the day wore on, and he continued to lie there: what was known about the Palace of Immortality? How long had the Possessors been there?

And that was all. And they were abstract questions now; for the time fold was up there in the future, and out of their reach. Any question about that was academic, would be interesting only because he had a strong curiosity. But no reply that either Johns or his daughter could give had a practical application.

Caxton visualized a future consisting of five, maybe six, conversations with Johns, and an occasional insult from Selanie; and he was appalled. . . . *Boy,* he thought, *there's got to be sex. Without that, I'll kill myself.*

With that thought, about midafternoon, he bestirred himself and went out of his room in search of the girl. The outer door was open; and he found that Johns had taken a metal chair of an odd kind, and was settling into it in the shade beside the trailer. What was odd about the chair was not obvious to Caxton, but Johns was reading and leaning back, and the chair was tilted so that he could do so comfortably. Caxton decided he would have to look that over to see the mechanical ingenuity of it. But that was for later.

What he said was, "Where's your daughter?"

"She went hunting," Johns said casually; but his body moved in a way which indicated that he didn't wish to be disturbed. His gaze remained glued to the book.

Hunting? Caxton walked past the seated man, on up the hill. The picture of the girl out there somewhere, alone, made him uneasy. By the time he had that thought, he was at the top of the shallow rise and gazing out over those distances. Though he scanned the horizon far and near, he couldn't see her anywhere.

At first, he tried to analyze his inability to notice her small, undoubtedly moving figure, as a problem in perspective. It was like being in a car looking for a parking space. At even a relatively near point, one often could not see that there were, in fact, two or three spaces available ahead. In the same way, there were, as he recalled it, small valleys, beginning a mile or so away, and many more valleys further on, that were invisible from where he stood.

She may have found a stream in one of those valleys, and be walking along it, trusting, he presumed, to some superior weapon that she carried, to protect her from any marauding band of Indians. What bothered him was that if Indians caught sight of her, they would most likely ambush her; and before she could even grab her weapon, would silently and from behind grab her and by achieving an instant overwhelm, make their capture.

He took off his coat, laid it on the grass and sat down beside it to watch for the girl. The sun sank lower in the sky; but not once did the girl emerge from one of the valleys. After at least an hour he began to doubt his memory . . . he did actually wander considerable distances. Maybe those valleys were much farther away than he believed, when he was exploring them in the twentieth and twenty-fifth centuries.

Presently the situation became incredible again. Because he could see a good five to eight miles in every direction—would she have walked that far?

Anxiously, Caxton called down to Johns. "I can't see your daughter anywhere, sir."

. "Oh, she took her bike," Johns called back, "and she's wearing her Fly-O; so she's all right." Having spoken, he returned to his reading.

Caxton felt deflated. Of course. How could he have forgotten? These people had had access to the remote future. The "bike" was probably as silent as the Fly-O, and maybe it too could fly.

He stood up. He put on his coat and walked down the hill, and so back to the trailer and his room. It was about an hour after that that he heard her voice. Instantly relieved, but also curious, Caxton hurried to the door. Standing in it, he saw the "bike." It was a three-wheeled device, and Selanie, wearing shorts, a halter, and a Fly-O, sat astride one part of it. At the moment that Caxton saw the thing, it was still several feet above the ground; and, clearly, it could fly. As he watched, the machine settled gracefully to the grass. Selanie got off, and now the closed-off part of the bike lifted up to reveal a capacious interior, which contained—as she took them out one by one—seven ducks, three more prairie chickens of the type he had seen the night before, and five rabbits.

Leaving the day's hunt lying on the ground, Selanie wheeled the machine toward the rear of the trailer and did three things. She pressed a button on the trailer, for an opening appeared in the trailer wall. Another button, and the bike began to fold itself. It was an amazing performance of folding, for in about a minute it had become a compact structure of flat surfaces folded against each other, and its total size seemed to be about two feet at its thickest. This structure Selanie lifted, as if it weighed nothing, into the recess that had opened in the trailer; which, as she drew back, closed, leaving only the faintest visible line.

She walked briskly back to where Caxton was gathering up the dead birds and rabbits. "Take them into the foreward storeroom," she commanded. "I'll clean them after dinner."

"I'll be glad to help," Caxton said.

But she rejected the offer with a curt shake of her head.

And that was the second day.

The next morning, when Caxton awakened, the trailer was in motion.

XXII

ALL THE TIME he was dressing, Caxton had to brace himself to keep from losing his balance. He went forward at last, and found father and daughter in the cab, Selanie driving.

The trailer, he saw, was moving slowly over relatively flat prairie—but it was not flat enough. Caxton settled awkwardly into the rear seat; several minutes went by before the woman saw him. Instantly, she took her foot off the accelerator and the big trailer came to a bumpy stop.

Selanie said, "You asked me the other day what you could do, Mr. Caxton. I'd like you to drive while I make breakfast."

It seemed like the first sign of improvement in their relationship. . . . As she crawled over the seat to where he was, he put his hand on her shoulder to steady her . . . and she made no comment. He removed the hand quickly the moment she was beside him. Then he stepped over into the driver's seat, and slid behind the wheel, searching the dashboard for the familiar mechanical devices of an automobile cab.

Since, except for the steering wheel, everything looked different, they had to show him. There were eight foot pedals, but he was soon able to put his foot lightly on the two that mattered: the brake and the accelerator. What the other pedals were for, he was not told; and he didn't experiment. Selanie left as soon as his driving lesson was completed; and Caxton found himself with her father in the seat beside him, and ahead of them a world without a single road, and moment by moment the need to make one decision after another as to what was the best pathless pathway for the big machine. He had had a vague idea of questioning Mr. Johns, but that was virtually impossible. All his attention and energy was needed for the task of driving.

Yet he finally managed to gasp, "Where are we going?"

The lean Johns shook his head. "You'll have to ask Selanie," he said. "It was her idea."

Some minutes later when they stopped for breakfast, Caxton had time to consider that. He thought then that this girl was quite a dominant type. The fact was, there were two men here who were not even being asked their opinions—on anything!

But at breakfast he asked, first, a question that had struck him when the purpose of the pedals was being explained.

"Can this trailer fly?"

"Yes."

Caxton was amazed. "Then why aren't we flying?"

"Because we have, unfortunately, a limited power supply." There was suddenly red color in her cheeks. "It's the one thing that I permitted a man—my father—to look after; but for some reason or other he kept neglecting to get a refill unit, trusting, I'm sure, to what he considered to be our perfect defensive position; not thinking of Bustaman persuading somebody like you to act against us. So here we are with power enough for two days of flying or about a year of driving."

"What kind of power is it?" Caxton asked.

"Something called adeledicnander," she said. "You

179

wouldn't know about that. It's powerful, but it must be periodically replaced."

So she wasn't aware that he had been to the twenty-fifth century. He had been wondering. Sitting there, Caxton remembered his disinterest up there in 2476 A.D. in learning the details of adeledicnander; now, they would all three pay the price of his ignorance and inattention.

Yet—and he brightened—it was also encouraging for his personal situation with Selanie. There would inevitably come a moment when they were at the end of the mechanical resources of their trailer. The sooner the better, he decided. Meaning, he thought grimly, the longer this trip, the better.

And so, his second main question was: "Where are we going?"

They were going, she said, where it would be easier to find food. "Toward the mountains, I would guess," she said. "I flew many hours yesterday, and saw very little game."

Caxton was silently glad to hear it. He had a feeling that a search for game could be a continuous moving process. He was still thinking about it, when Selanie said, "If you don't mind, Mr. Caxton, I think we should get Father in and start up again."

Caxton drove the rest of that day, and the days that followed, with a faint, satisfied smile on his face and a smug feeling. He invariably took the most roundabout routes, always on the grounds of seeking the flattest land over which to maneuver their bulky machine. Several times Selanie sat beside him. On each occasion, she urged him to fly over certain rough areas, suggesting that it would save fuel. (She had shown him late that first afternoon how to fly the trailer.) And once she actually took the wheel away from him, and flew over a wooded area that he had intended to go around. Finally, on the thirty-fifth day of the journey, she informed him curtly that she would henceforth do the driving.

The fourth morning after that, the trailer did not resume its journey. At breakfast Selanie announced, "We'll stay here for a while."

"Here," as Caxton discovered when he went outside, was in the lower Rockies—he guessed near where Colorado Springs or Denver, or perhaps even Pueblo, would someday be. The trailer was drawn up beside a mountain stream that glistened brightly in the sun. As he stood there, gazing about him at the rock-strewn hillside, Caxton suddenly realized that the girl had come out of the trailer and was standing nearby.

He turned and she said, without looking directly at him, "Mr. Caxton, I have been thinking about our situation here in this era. And it seems wrong that my father and I should have to associate so intimately with the person who caused such a disaster, and whose method of driving—let me say it frankly—suddenly brought me the feeling that he was trying to use up our fuel."

Her expression as she spoke was not antagonistic. She was wearing slacks and a blouse. The slacks were red, the blouse white—very pretty. Not antagonistic, but her words came to Caxton with a terrible shock.

Before he could recover his wits, she finished, "And so, I'm wondering if we couldn't supply you with some weapons, and some equivalent of a tent, and have you leave. I don't mean today, but as soon as you can brace yourself to be man enough."

After a long moment, Caxton realized that his principal emotion was amazement. Because where could he go?

The thought was so powerful that he actually turned away from her and gazed out at this remote world again as if to verify that it was indeed an uninhabited wilderness. The girl (woman?) and he were standing beside the swift-flowing stream, and everything was wild and untouched, and, most convincing of all, in his mind was the knowledge of all the miles they had driven, the forests and rivers they had flown over. And, once again, there was no question. This was western America before the coming of civilization.

Slowly, he faced Selanie again. He wondered if her father had concurred in this confrontation. And doubted it. In spite of himself a smile touched his lips at the realization that was suddenly in his mind: *It takes a woman*, he thought, *to tell a man to get out under such circumstances.*

Just like that, on impulse, he spoke the thought aloud. The girl flushed a little, but when she spoke it was in an even voice, "I have a lot of experience, Mr. Caxton, and so I'm only too sadly familiar with the kind of thinking that goes on in the mind of the paranoid-type male. And so"—she shrugged—"I'd just not rather face that situation at some future time."

In spite of himself, her words penetrated. He had thought that his barriers were up, but he was staggered by the cruel meaning. Paranoid! . . . She was really letting him have it.

Nonetheless, he was presently able to protest: "Look! what I did was designed to get me into the Palace of Immortality. I can't"—stubbornly—"see anything wrong with that. The truth is, you people had no business withholding it from me once I found out about it. So you were the villains, not me. But"—he felt a lot better by the time he had this twisted thought—"I don't sense

182

any repugnance in myself to having you two in close proximity to me."

The girl said coldly, "Your feelings are not at issue. You're the intruder."

It was still attack, and still without mercy. Yet he was a man who had always been able to hold his own with women, and somehow not be bowled over when they did their outrageous acts. At least, not bowled over for long.

This particular female madness triggered a kind of facetiousness in him. The instant that happened, he was secure again within himself. He said, "Any time you have a method for me to go up to the future, I'll be glad to go."

"I'm afraid," she said stiffly, "that kind of solution will be impossible—thanks to you. So now that you know my thoughts, what do you suggest?"

He was a man who had been for too long a time without a woman in 2476 A.D. And now more than a month here. So he was ready. He said, "There are two ways of facing the future here, and I can assure you that yours is wrong."

"Mr. Caxton," Selanie said sharply, "I do not wish to hear your solution."

He couldn't have stopped himself. He said simply, "If we're going to be in this predicament from now on, you become my wife. And I do all the hard work, as a man should."

She laughed. It was a tinkling laughter that could have been musical, but it had a cutting, derisive note in it, and it ended only as she said, "Incredible. Evidently, Mr. Caxton, you don't know that you have a continuing unpleasant odor."

Caxton felt the color drain from his cheeks. The shock

was all the greater because he had forgotten. With his return to the twentieth century, and then to the seventeenth, the memory of that unhappy experience in the twenty-fifth century had gone off into some nether part of his brain.

In his anguish, he was only vaguely aware that she had turned away from him, and was climbing the hill that overlooked the swift-flowing stream. Her departure took the awful pressure off of him. And so, presently, he watched her, thinking: *She's a live person, with her own needs. So there has got to come a time when even I—odor and all—will look good to her.*

Standing there, watching her as she now reached the top of the hill, he wondered if—when that time came and suddenly the resistance was gone out of her and she was willing—he would then just peacefully accept what she offered; would he act as if all those minutes and hours and months of waiting while nature brought her to her senses, were not to be held against her? Sullenly he guessed that he could. But there would be mental reservations, he realized, bitterly. That was why a woman often lost a man's respect: because she never used her God-given brains.

The bitter reflections stopped. For Selanie was precipitately running back down the hill. The speed of her return alarmed him . . . something wrong! Involuntarily, Caxton started toward her. She waved him back urgently. Moments later, she arrived beside him, breathless.

"Indians!" she said. "Dozens of them."

"Did they see you?"

"I think so."

XXIII

By THE TIME they were in the trailer and had the door closed, Caxton had a satiric reaction. How odd for her to have taken flight just like any normal person. . . . What about that high-and-mighty attitude which she had expressed to him so insultingly about Indians being peaceful?

He discreetly spoke none of these thoughts, but silently went with her to the cab window—and sat there beside her as about a hundred Indian males came racing around a bend in the stream, and halted in confusion, those behind almost falling over their companions. In fact several fell, and several were pushed down.

A dozen moments went by. Caxton realized with a faint shock that he had stopped breathing. It cost him an effort to exhale and then inhale. Finally, he thought, *They look exactly like a painting by George Catlin. So in two hundred years up to the time of the famous artist, the clothes didn't change . . . hard to imagine how they could in a society that lacked the scientific or philosophical roots of potential progress.*

At that instant, Mr. Johns settled into the rear seat. He chuckled. "I've activated the brain sound. After all, we don't really want them spying on us or prowling around here."

The "brain sound," as he explained it, created a humming effect in the human brain toward which it was directed—which really meant that it disturbed the inner ear in a nondirectional manner.

The effect was visible out there. The Indians were retreating. First they turned and walked slowly away, as if striving to maintain their male dignity. Then they walked faster, as if by mutual consent dignity was replaced by a strong survival impulse. Abruptly, they broke into a scampering run, and, running, disappeared around the bend. Caxton went outside after a while. He was jittery but he felt he should be the one. He climbed the hill, and from its height he caught a few glimpses of stragglers in the distance along the stream. They were, he was relieved to see, still running.

When he came down, Selanie had gone to her room, but Johns was still in the cab. Caxton sank down beside him and asked, "How far does that, uh, brain sound, project?"

Johns shrugged. "It's line of sight. So only while they were in view. After all, we don't want to hurt these people."

He seemed friendly for the first time. And Caxton, who had suddenly had an idea, took advantage of the opportunity and asked about the instrument. "Can this thing that produces the brain sound be reduced to hand-weapon size?"

Johns's answer was to put his hand into his pocket and carefully draw out a tiny metallic object. With his other hand, he grasped Caxton's palm, squeezed the fingers back and placed the object in it.

"Don't point it at your own head," he advised.

The object was slightly less than half an inch in diameter; and it was a little difficult to determine which was the part that could "point." But Caxton held it steady in his hand exactly the way it had been placed, and then he carefully bent down to it and studied it. Seen close up, it showed as an intricate structure, each protuberance of which, at Caxton's request, Johns explained.

The device, it seemed, was always on. But it operated, literally, on line of sight. The slightest barrier, other than the gaseous atmosphere, stopped its action. A piece of transparent tissue paper was a complete barrier. "So, if you're ever out and you run into a life form you want to drive off," said the older man, "just take it out of your pocket, point it correctly, and they'll be confused and run."

Caxton was struck by the wording. "You're giving this to me?" he asked.

"Of course. We should all carry one."

As Caxton slipped the object into his own pocket, he realized that an enormous and satisfying thought had suddenly come into view over the horizon of his mind. He said, "A few minutes ago, your daughter asked me to leave the trailer—since I was an intruder. For the first time, I can see how to do so. With this device, I can probably go and live with those Indians."

He mustered a smile in his need to hide the sly impulse that was motivating him. "After all," he continued in a hearty tone, "it would be wrong of me to force my presence indefinitely on people whom I have injured as I have you and your daughter, particularly since"—he concluded suavely—"your daughter has informed me I have an unpleasant odor."

The older man nodded. "I've noticed," he said. "It's a one-way time travel odor, and I've been wondering how you acquired it."

Caxton, who had parted his lips to continue with his sly game, closed them again. And then he sat there.

When he came out of that shock, he found that he was explaining to Johns about his five-hundred-year journey to far Centaurus.

As he came to that awareness he stopped, startled at himself. For nearly two months he had successfully suppressed the need to communicate his secret. It was not that he had any reason to hold it back. It was simply that he had a lifetime policy of never communicating anything for the sake of telling it.

He forgot that. It seemed minor. He echoed, "A time smell?" Pause, then: "Does Selanie know?"

Johns shook his head. There was a faraway expression in his eyes. "That," he said, "was quite a long journey. Too bad. You'll have to live an undetermined number of years in the Palace to balance that off. I know of no other that was longer than a hundred years."

"Why didn't you tell your daughter?"

Johns was astonished. "Why should I?"

Caxton was outraged. . . . What was the matter with this guy? Didn't he even talk to his own relatives? The brief passion ceased. He remembered how uncommunicative Johns had been; and there was no doubt, he didn't talk much to anyone.

Johns's attention was no longer directly on Caxton. His mood had become sort of—"Well, well, so I keep running into repercussions of my experiment. So Bustaman brought him all the way down from the twenty-fifth century to defeat me and my dream." The probabilities would most likely go on. They were too numerous for Bustaman to stop. But the experimental aspect was doomed. Johns shook his head wonderingly, and thought— How can someone who is less, be better? It was a question that Claudan Johns had asked himself many times. On occasion, when he had looked around at all the bright, wonderful Possessors whom he had created and saw how bright and wonderful they were, and how completely they had become the New People of whose existence he had dreamed his dream of perfection, it seemed incredible that they accepted themselves for what they were without question. He also could see them for what they were, and appreciate them —and be glad that they didn't think about it. But it was equally obvious that anybody who didn't think about himself, even though perfect, was not—what? He wasn't sure what.

I am not perfect, he thought, *but I can think about myself, and also observe them with dispassionate awareness. So I am the experimenter, and they are my subjects. But they are better.*

He had never participated. He watched while they gaily went off into probability worlds, willingly creating duplicates of themselves, and never seemed to worry about how it would all come out. Claudan Johns worried. And he never duplicated *himself.*

But they were better, freer, more capable, happier, more intelligent. It was amazing. They were better, and he was less. But in his studies he had learned things that they had never been motivated to find out—they just lived it; they didn't have to know it—and so he was tolerated, and in a curious fashion accepted as the mentor and leader.

In that same dispassionate fashion, he had studied Peter Caxton . . . a paranoid type, he observed, by twentieth century nomenclature. It was estimated by the Possessors that twenty percent of twentieth century males were paranoid in the way that Caxton was. Dominant, subjective, self-centered, on the personal level incapable of seeing another point of view. It was a type of male who—the Possessors believed from their study of history—had once been around in even greater percentages. The total gradually increased going backward in time until, among pre-Dawn men, it was about eighty percent. It was never one hundred percent. Never. There were always some men around who could be reasoned with. On the personal level, the Peter Caxton type could not be reasoned with.

The dream of the New People was that, in the future, there must be no Peter Caxtons. And, of course, no Kameel Bustamans.

So Claudan Johns saw with a certain compassion, of which he was capable, that the quest of Peter Caxton was not possible. The Possessors, obsessed by *their* quest, could not accept him.

Yet, Johns saw his own daughter was disturbed by Caxton. . . . Maybe it was the knowledge in her mind that they couldn't get out of there. Perhaps a long-buried womanly instinct was stirring. Historically, women had associated with the more subjective males . . . like Caxton. The fact that this woman was his own daughter was no problem to Claudan Johns. She was, after all, 439 years old, and, it said somewhere in his mind, she was capable of looking after herself.

As these thoughts completed themselves in his mind, he rose to his feet with an enigmatic smile. "Don't go off to those Indians," he said, "until I've had a chance to discuss this matter with Selanie."

Caxton, who had no intention of going off anywhere, and whose sole purpose in bringing up the Indians was so that Selanie *would* hear about it, promised that he would take no hasty action.

But the days went by and nothing happened except that Johns was more friendly. As a result they had a number of conversations, and Caxton learned a few—a tiny few—more pieces of information about the Palace of Immortality.

Of how the foldback in time occurred in November of 9812 A.D., and went in reverse to February, 1977, and then presumably started forward again. But they had not found where it went after that.

Not, Caxton thought, *that it mattered to people sealed off in the seventeenth century.*

On another occasion Johns described how the hope of the Possessors was that they would be able to find a probability way of going forward after 9812 A.D. "I told them that the tests I've made show that there is no sweet by-and-by, that it's all here, and that the only future is in the probabilities in this vast vault of nearly eight thousand years—between 1977 and 9812. That, and nothing more, is the time universe."

"What tests did you make?" asked Caxton, the physicist in him stirring momentarily.

Smilingly, Johns shook his head.

In still another conversation, Caxton asked, "How did you happen to let Bustaman into your experiment?"

"The same way all the real Possessors came in," was the reply. "A small percentage of individuals unknowingly have the ability to go through time. That was my great discovery. As soon as I knew what the factor was, I started my long search for people who possessed it. Meanwhile, in one of my own time transformations I had discovered the Palace. And so I was finally ready for the great experiment, because in the Palace I could use people who were not themselves Possessors."

"Let me understand you," said Caxton. "There are two aspects here. One is that people who could of themselves go through time existed naturally in the world?"

"Yes."

"As a result of your ability as a Possessor," Caxton continued, "and this is a second and separate aspect, you accidentally discovered the Palace of Immortality."

"That's correct."

"The Palace was empty when you found it?" asked Caxton.

"Yes. Empty. Deserted. We might suspect it was used for a long time, and then abandoned. Abandoned for what? There's no clue."

A little later that same day, Caxton ran into Johns in the corridor of the trailer. Johns said, "Your question about Bustaman—I've been thinking about him since. In his zeal, he made some interesting discoveries. He was the first to make me aware that entire probability worlds could be merged after they had been separated for a long time. For example, that probability of 2083 A.D., where you were. That was my group's first attempt to create an idyllic everybody-loves-everybody Earth. It took Bustaman a long time, but by 2130 A.D. he had located all—at least enough—of the metal objects, and brought them back to the Palace. As the two worlds merged there was some confusion but nothing desperate."

Caxton had tried to follow a visual concept of what Johns was saying. But the picture of two probability worlds merging was too much for him. The implication was that most people had, except for some emotional variations, been substantially in the same places, had essentially gone the same directions, and, at the moment of merging, were at the exact same spot in both probability worlds. . . . His mind boggled at that, but could not find a point of acceptance.

Those people in that alternate probability world of

2083 A.D. really had tried to help him. His hysteria had been disturbing to persons he impinged on. But, it was clear now, their pursuit of him had never been threatening, and in the final issue he had probably escaped because they didn't force their assistance on anyone.

Caxton came out of his private thoughts to realize that Johns had walked on and disappeared into his laboratory. Caxton shrugged. Such conversations had, he realized, a false interest. Such things didn't matter. Here in 1653 A.D. everything that had happened in that out-of-reach future was abstract and pointless.

He was sitting at the breakfast table the next morning with that negative thought still in his mind. It was raining outside, a singularly dull sound. Caxton visualized a thousand miles of rain out there—and thirty years of nothing here in this trailer.

Boy, he thought, *I'd better do something . . . but what?* Only the future interested him, and his quest for immortality. Yet maybe he had better make his peace with the present, and actually seek out the Indians, as he had threatened.

The thought was like a cue. He looked up at the woman. "Did your father tell you about my plan to live with the Indians?"

The girl turned and stared at him. She seemed particularly fresh and young looking; Caxton felt an instant longing. "Yes," she said.

"That's a good idea, isn't it, all things considered?"

The woman was silent; then: "What would you do there?" she asked.

Caxton pretended astonishment. "Live a normal life, for heaven's sake. Persuade one of their women to live with me the way—"

He stopped. He had been about to say, "The way you once lived with me."

His thought poised. He trembled.

For all of these numerous days, it had been apparent that this, here, in the trailer, was her earliest awareness of him; and that therefore (he thought of the corollary for the very first time) the time up there in the Palace of Immortality when he had awakened in the bed beside an older Selanie, *must be later.*

The implication was that for there to be a *later,* they *must have gotten out of this predicament.*

Something of his terrible excitement as that realization came to him must have shown in his face. Selanie said, "What's the matter?"

He told her in a shaking voice, so caught up in his own inner disturbance that he noticed her first reaction only vaguely.

For a moment, her face showed—something. . . . Then she seemed to steady herself. It was not just a body steadiness, but the sound of it was in her voice when she spoke.

"I don't remember such a probability. So it must have been one that Price created of me for you without my knowledge. I'll ask Father about it. I'm convinced that Bustaman once created a probability of Father without his knowledge." She looked at him with the same steadiness. "You didn't happen to run into Dad somewhere along the line?"

"No, sorry." Caxton's high hope had already dropped in the face of her deflating attitude and words; and her final question disturbed him. He asked, astonished, "Why would Bustaman do a thing like that?"

"He has a terrible false pride," she said. "I'm sure he felt that only he has pure motives; and so, when he discovered that Father had remained outside of the experiment, I'm sure he had to try to—" She stopped. "Never mind that. Tell me again exactly what happened between me and you."

Caxton's heart was no longer in the story. Nonetheless, he gave her the account, in detail this time. But all the time that he was speaking, he was thinking: *I've just had a glimpse of the struggle between the two opposing forces in the Palace of Immortality, even though one of them was only one man.*

He realized that he was feeling terribly cynical.

It seemed as if only human beings could have arrived at the quarrel that divided Bustaman from the main group occupying the Palace of Immortality. Surely, no greater insanity could be imagined. These people controlled a twist in time where, for all practical purposes, time went backward. Thus they could undo upon their own persons the years accumulated in the main timestream—undo them over and over and over again. And, incredibly, this had become an issue of violence.

That intense feeling came to an end, because, as he finished his retelling of his experience in the Palace, he had a thought, and he said, "All right. Now you tell me something. How come that probability Selanie married me?"

The girl laughed. "One of these days I'll have to have Father explain the probability thing to you. Then you'll understand."

"But what I've just told you," said Caxton, disappointed, "doesn't mean anything?"

"I'll talk to Dad about it," she said, and her voice was steady again, "and he can explain that to you, also."

With those words, he came back from his hope and was mentally again in the trailer with the dull sound of the rain, and the drab future of nothing as his only prospect. "Okay, okay," he said, wearily, "what about the Indians? When shall I leave?"

He stopped because the girl had turned away, and his final words were addressed to her retreating back. If she made any answer to his questions, Caxton did not hear it. Glumly, he got up and went back to his room and lay down.

All right, he thought, *so that little game isn't going to work. So maybe I will actually go and live with the Indians.*

Try as he would, he couldn't really imagine *that*.

He dozed, and awakened to the sound of rain. He slept again, and when he came to, there was the rain. . . .

Somewhere in there, he ate two more meals to the sound of rain.

And, somewhere in there, the fantastic thought came that they would have to get out of this time. It seemed ridiculous to have such a purpose even come into his mind. Not here, in this wilderness. For, surely, there was no way *up* from an era that had no civilized people in it except themselves. But he had it. And it kept coming back. And he kept telling himself that up there in the 1970's it had been impossible; yet it had happened. So, by that reasoning, it could happen also in the seventeenth century.

That night, in the darkness of his own tiny room, he lay awake, arguing with the scientific part of his brain, with his training as a physicist.

Of course, he told himself with a faint smile, *I'm only an M.A. . . . and it was well-known that M.A.'s were still permitted a tiny amount of madness.* They could still mingle with the people; even contemplate an occasional unproved hypothesis, without—and this was important—guilt. A fellow student at college who, like Caxton, was going to have to drop out and get a job, had even tried to persuade his friends that an M.A. status was actually better; because an M.A. was still entitled to have some fun.

Thus reassured, Caxton continued to consider the impossible hope that had so suddenly flashed into his mind: that there had to be a way of getting back to the future.

What presently astonished him was that, with the reaffirmation of his real goal, came the thought that he had to stop badgering that poor girl.

The fact was, there was no logical reason which said that Selanie Johns should satisfy the sex needs of Peter Caxton, or of any other man she didn't like.

With that realization, something inside him relaxed enormously.

This time when he slept, he did not awaken until morning. He was about to turn over with a groan, when he realized that the rain sound had ceased. And when, after hastily dressing, he went out, the door was open; and through it fell a generous spray of brilliant sunshine.

Caxton stepped gingerly down to grass that sparkled with wetness and saw that Claudan Johns was walking toward him alongside the swollen river that had been a mountain stream. The older man waved, and Caxton said, "Where's your daughter, sir?"

"Oh, she's left," said Johns.

It was a strange way of saying that she had gone off on her bike. Caxton felt his first ever-so-slight return of irritation with Selanie. He shook his head, thinking: *Whenever I zig, she zags. Just when I'm ready to declare peace, she's gone off somewhere. . . .* So, that by the time she came back, who knew what new emotional disturbance he would be in in relation to her?

He grew resigned. . . . *Okay, so that's the way she is. I'd better get used to it.*

"Selanie has some idea," continued Johns, "that Bustaman—of all people—maneuvered me into a probability world once for self-esteem reasons, without my knowing it. If that's true, then I can be rescued also."

The conversation was making less and less sense. Caxton's impression was that he was being subjected to technical chitchat, as if he understood the basic principles and could therefore fit in the missing pieces. And, of course, he could do nothing of the kind.

He suppressed an impulse to go back into the trailer. Suppressed it because, damn it, there was nothing to do inside. He thought finally, wearily: *All right, so I want to remain outside and be here when she flies back in. It would be a little ridiculous not to admit that to himself. So I'll keep on talking.*

Aloud, he said, "This whole probability business is very mysterious. Apparently I'm up there in a couple of probability worlds myself.

Johns shook his head. "They won't work," he said firmly. "We tested it while you were sleeping, and evidently what Price told you was true. You were too rigid for the probability aspect to affect you. I thought the accumulated time energy in your cells might help, but that doesn't change the you's up there. Too bad."

Caxton was parting his lips to continue with another association of his own, when it occurred to him: *What this guy just said makes no sense. In fact, for several minutes I haven't understood anything he said.*

Caxton began, "I beg your pardon, sir, this conversation seems to have passed me by. Is it all right if we start again?"

Johns gave him a startled look.

Caxton hesitated; then: "*What* did you do to me in my sleep?"

Johns was calm again. "We tried to merge you from here with one of those probability you's." He shrugged. "It didn't take for the reasons, no doubt, that Price gave you. Too bad."

"Merge me?" echoed Caxton. He had an awful, sinking sensation.

"I seem to remember something about this now," Johns chattered on. "About fifty years ago in my life—" He broke off, apologetically. "I'm in and out of the Palace, living somewhere for a while adding years to my life, and then taking them off again. Fortunately, there's never been any hurry. Past time, you know, waits forever for those who can move freely through time. . . . So, anyway," he continued, "I'm reminded that Price had me go back in time and set up an early probability for somebody from his teen period before 1977. So then I went up to that same person at age thirty—that was in the later 1960's—picked him up and took him forward in time and handed him over to Price. Afterward, Price told me that they were unable to merge the older with the younger in terms of personality, but that the younger had to be merged with the older, and that the merging had no effect on the older. After what you told Selanie, I suddenly realized that must have been you." He was apologetic again. "Such details tend to slip away from the forefront of the mind."

He finished, "Anyway, that's still the problem. Before I merged Selanie with the Selanie probability you told her about, she suggested I try it on you—but yours didn't work, as I told you. And that's too bad. You see, if she's right about Bustaman having created a probability of me, then if I merged with up there, you'd be left here alone. That bothered Selanie," said Claudan Johns.

XXIV

GLANDS CAN ONLY be stimulated so long; fear fades into apathy; shock can renew so many times only.

At last the man about to be hanged climbs up to the gallows, and stands there dully. When the trap door is sprung, he does not even notice the exact moment.

A parallel darkness descended on Caxton's mind for a timeless period after Claudan Johns's words hit him with their meaning.

During the entire trauma, Johns kept talking; and what finally penetrated of that continuing monologue was, ". . . If you want to take the chance, we'll have to hurry. Selanie said she would allow ten days before she merged me."

It sounded like nonsense, but the sense did come through finally. Caxton nodded. For the first time he was aware of a vague bitterness. At least it was an emotion and not physiologic devastation. The feeling took no form, pointed at no one; simply lay there in his body like the first stirring of return of consciousness.

"I'll make breakfast," he said at that point. He added, "And I might as well find out how the trailer equipment works, since I'll be here alone."

He turned, and went inside; and he was busily doing what he had often seen Selanie do with the cooking utensils, when a thought touched him. He had no recollection of going in search of Johns but there he was suddenly standing in the laboratory doorway, and saying, "If you merge with another Claudan Johns up there, you'll recover your ability to move through time. Why don't you come back for me then?"

"That'll be a different probability world," said Johns, "so I wouldn't know how to get back here."

"For God's sake," exploded Caxton, "this is the real world. You've got to get back to it sooner or later."

There was a long silence. The lean man had straightened. His gray eyes, flecked with tiny darknesses, gazed into Caxton's haunted face. "Peter," he said soberly, "you don't understand. There is no real world. You evidently haven't grasped the enormousness of what we're dealing with. I thought you told Selanie that Price had described the probability thing to you. Listen! There are an *infinite* number of probability worlds. That's one of our difficulties. For example, we can't find the timefold when it presumably starts forward again in 1977, and we can't find anything that goes forward after 9812 A.D. where the backfold begins. So far as we know, the world ends November fourteenth of that year on every probability."

Startled, Caxton parted his lips to say, "But that's ridiculous. Obviously, the world goes on." He didn't say it, because it was suddenly not so obvious.

Finally, a logical sequence occurred to him, and he said lamely, "How does your daughter expect to discover that accidental probability of you?"

"Oh." Johns had started to bend again over a long, transparent box that he had on the floor of the trailer. At Caxton's question, he straightened once more and he said, "Let's see if we can't get this all clear for you. There are two clues. One is something Bustaman said before he made his break with us. He said that he was

202

now—at that time—the only Possessor without a probability self somewhere. When somebody pointed at me, he merely laughed significantly and refused to discuss it. Selanie believes that he had a paranoid need to put me in the wrong and to satisfy himself that his ideal was an exclusive condition." The older man's eyes sought to fixate Caxton. He asked, "Got it that far?"

He was being spoken to as if he were a six-year-old, but maybe—Caxton smiled wanly as he recalled the vague period since he had first heard of Selanie "leaving"—maybe he deserved it.

Johns went on, "The second clue is, one of our people told my daughter that she had seen me in a probability world. Selanie is going to find out from that woman where this was. The women will go there, and give the information to that Claudan Johns, whereupon he will merge me, and then *that* will be me. So the next time I come back to the seventeenth century, it won't be in this probability world; it will be in that one, and you're not in that one. So you'd better just do what I suggested."

The bitterness was back. It was an actual taste in Caxton's mouth; and this time he had a thought with it: *Really, Selanie owes me nothing. So why does it bother me that she left?* It was not so much that he missed her, but there was a criticism in him of himself for having importuned her when, in fact, his every word was a nuisance to her.

An hour later, Caxton thought grimly of an historical parallel to Selanie's departure: Even the Black Plague had its good side—for the survivors. Suddenly, people who had never had any rights, who had never owned anything, and who had not even had a hope of affluence

—suddenly they were heirs to bits and pieces and lumps of property.

So, he thought, *I guess as a starter, I get the bike.*

Johns was in his laboratory busy with something; and so there was no one to deny Caxton as he manipulated the machine out of its fold-in, pressed the button as he had seen Selanie do, and watched it set itself up. A minute later, he was astride it, gliding through the air, heading upstream.

He looked down on a three-dimensional wilderness that was as fascinating to watch as playing solitaire hour after hour. Distance. Mountains. Streams. Blue sky. Clouds. . . . Don't get too far away. Know your landmarks. . . .

The same game of solitaire in flight was his during the next day, and the next.

Came the fourth morning after Selanie's departure. After breakfast, Johns stood up from the little table and said, "Any time you want to come into my lab and see what I'm busy with, you're welcome. I'll be glad to explain it."

Caxton muttered a thank you. But he didn't move. And the memory of the invitation faded as Johns walked through the doorway.

Sometime during that day, as he took the bike and flew off to his hours-long reverie in motion, Caxton asked himself: *Is it possible that I can continue in this semiconscious state for the entire ten days?*

It turned out that he had lost count of the days. Twice, on what must have been the tenth morning, he called to Johns to come and get breakfast.

Silence replied, except for a faint echo of his own voice.

"Hey!" whispered Caxton. "You're not gone?"

He was talking to himself.

Caxton went outside. The mental numbness of the past ten days seemed to be extending to his body; for he was standing in the icy stream, wet almost to the waist, before he realized that he had unseeingly walked straight into the water.

Sobered, he waded ashore. *That's all I need,* he thought. *Catch a cold and die of pneumonia.*

About noon, when he was still waiting for his trousers, shoes and socks to dry in the sun, it struck him that all his problems were internal, for the man who owned— as he now did—the combination super-trailer-truck-airplane, in all this land there was nothing physical to worry about. And he was good for a balance of ninety years.

He had to make a decision. That was it. A decision. About what?

As darkness settled slowly over the wilderness universe of a primitive America, he still didn't have the faintest idea. Except that, as a strictly practical matter, he was inside the trailer with the door firmly secured against . . . fear. He admitted the fear to himself without shame.

In spite of his anxiety, he fell asleep instantly.

It had been a clear day, and yet the first time he awakened, he heard the sound of rain on the trailer roof. Once more, sleep came easily. He awakened to two awarenesses.

It had stopped raining. That was one. The second: he realized what his decision must be. He was a man— he had to face it now, as he had faced it in the past— who blew his mind just about every hour on the hour. It was a handicap that would have put most people into a permanent spin. But somehow he had rescued his wounded ego each time, and carefully tucked it back into his head and he had thereafter, each time, counted his winnings.

I haven't counted my winnings, he thought now. The fantastic trailer, with all the things in it that he had never more than glanced at in passing.

He realized he was wide awake. His watch said nine minutes after three as he entered Claudan Johns's laboratory. Instantly, and for the first time, he realized it was the largest room in the huge vehicle, and that it was beyond all question the most compact scientific workroom he had ever seen.

A few minutes of tentative checking verified that every spare inch of wall was utilized for some fold-in of the same complexity as Selanie's bike. And each fold-in was itself a structure designed to do many things. The largest item was a heavy lead-lined projecting mechanism which occupied a portion of one wall and had a book of instructions soldered to its base. The book opened on the sensational statement: "Manufactures all 154 elements from air. (Warning: will produce no radio-active materials unless certain special preconditions are met—see page 98).

Caxton backed away from those words—*literally* took several steps back. His intent was to study the remarkable machine. What happened was, in his final backward step he stumbled over the coffin-like box on the floor, and half-fell, half-knelt to save himself.

Crouched there, he saw the letter lying on the bottom of the box. On its face was written: "For Peter Caxton."

Opening it and snatching out the contents was the act of moments. The contents consisted of several sheets of paper with a covering letter.

Caxton climbed to his feet and carried the letter over

to a fold-down table beside a chair. He intended to sit down and read it, but the first words had already grabbed his attention. He stood there, then, and read the letter from beginning to end.

Dear Peter C:
I can well understand your reluctance to undertake what in your era—the late twentieth century —was still an experimental method. What I want to say is that, with the power available in this vehicle, and the environment which it makes possible, you can feel reassured. Thus, with temperature control absolutely guaranteed (so long as the trailer itself is not destroyed by the elements—and I suggest a cave as the best place to make certain that doesn't happen), you have my assurance that the equipment will take you as far as you want to go. However, I recommend for you either the twentieth century (1979) or 2476 A.D. Don't go anywhere else, is my advice. Selanie and I are agreed that you are not stable enough emotionally to be able to withstand a foray into another era. I regret to inform you that we (Selanie and I) are also agreed that the Possessors will not accept you into the Palace of Immortality. Still, it's your choice where you go. Just make sure you survive.

Claudan Johns

The attached sheets consisted of drawings—which Caxton quickly identified as being connected with the transparent coffin on the floor—and a fairly technical description of machinery which would perform various functions. One arrow finally grabbed his attention, for it pointed at a container and said, "Blood drains in here and is frozen"!

Caxton sat down suddenly in the chair; and as he now rapidly read the other items, with a jump of comprehension he abruptly came to a gulping reality.

Cryonics!

But that was unproved.

It took a while, then, to get back to Claudan Johns's letter, with its certainties. It took longer to make up his mind; yet in the end his reason was the same: For a man with *his* purposes, what else was there to do?

The faint light of dawn was breaking in the east as Caxton opened the outer door and stepped down to the rain-wet grass. Later, he ate an uneasy breakfast, but he realized he was waiting for daylight and that waiting is hard when you know at last what you intend to do.... He intended to look for a suitable cave.

When he found it, on the third day, he flew over and carefully backed the trailer in. It required another day to block off the front of the cave. But at last the job was done. He took off his clothes and lay down in the bottom of the coffin.

What he did next would have been easier if he had had a helper, but the equipment was there. The instructions had been to insert four of the needles into his legs and two into his left arm. Caxton winced with each needle insert, but as in 2476 A.D., the insertion was not painful, it was the anticipation that hurt, not the needle.

It took a while to tape each needle into position with the special material provided; that was very important, Johns had written.

But the job was finally completed, and Caxton lay back gingerly and carefully drew the cover down into position and locked it into place.

The instructions had said, "Once the cover is down, don't waste any oxygen. Continue with the next step immediately."

But he couldn't help it. He reached up for the button that would start the "process" of time travel by freezing. And there, finger touching the button, he stopped.

Am I crazy? he asked himself.

For God's sake, this will be my second trip into a distant time. . . . Somehow, the journey by way of the Palace of Immortality didn't have the same stark reality.

Once again, it was a case of the wheels of his mind spinning in a vacuum. For even as he had the holding-back thoughts, his finger, driven by an obstinacy that had no give in it, pushed.

He heard a click.

What happened next was not quite as he would have anticipated, if he had considered that there might be anything but blankness (which he hadn't). Somewhere, somebody said in astonishment, "I felt a distance call from below. Check fast, all you tuners." There was a pause, and then another voice—a woman's—said, "It's not a call. It's an energy flow." A third voice—that of a second man—said, "But from where? It feels a long way off." Once more, the woman spoke: "A man's body has broken the barrier. . . ." The voices began to recede. Like whispers, they became progressively less identifiable as being male or female: ". . . It's a dead body—feels like . . ." Now someone else: "Not really dead; frozen. . . . Yes—" Another voice: "But artificially. . . . Oh, one of those; they don't normally show that strong. . . . This one starts with enough, so he'll make it. . . . All right, trace him—"

For a time after that they seemed to be still whispering, but there was no longer any sound that Caxton could identify. Presently the shadow whispering also ended.

Caxton tried to open his eyes—and couldn't.

Stiff—that was the feeling that his body communicated to him . . . Don't move!

He didn't.

XXV

IF SOMEONE knew that on the night of September tenth, 2476 A.D., at about eleven P.M., a Peter Caxton went aboard the aircraft of Kameel Bustaman and went off somewhere—and if Peter Caxton walked into the hotel at midnight that same night, there would be no problems of confusion of identity.

And this time, Caxton told himself, there would be no nonsense. He would go on that trip with Renfrew and Blake; and, while on it, *learn* the science of this era.

Actually, he used one of the trailer's Fly-O's, and landed on the little Fly-O balcony of his own room. He went inside, gulping a little at the perfection of it all.

But Johns had been right: the trailer equipment was superb. He had set the timing of it for September third, giving himself a week to recuperate. By the fifth day, he was chafing for action. But he had resisted his impatience; and here he was.

I'll take that trip. Then I'll come back here, and discover from the research firm the present home of Daniel Magoelson—and take it from there.

The beauty of it was all that fantastic experience, but here in this room he had a replacement keep-the-odor-in suit, and so he could go downstairs tomorrow, and nobody would suspect.

It was not, it developed, quite like that. In a universe

211

of sharp observers, there was that sharp observer, Ned Blake, who took one long, speculative look at Caxton the next morning and said, "You've changed. What happened?"

Caxton was curious. "Changed—how?"

"You look like the cat that has caught the mouse," said Blake, "and is not going to share it."

"I'd have thought," replied Caxton glibly, "that it'd be the other way around. I've finally decided to make my peace with this era, go on that trip with Jim and you—peacefully—and not be thinking of where else I should be, which is what I've been doing."

"Well." Blake stared at him doubtfully. "I guess that could be it. But there's a different expression in your eyes and face. If I didn't know better, I'd say that you've become a tougher type. More like you know where you're going."

Caxton was silent, a little startled. He'd been a winner, he thought, he'd taken chances. He had made the decision to risk another dangerous trip to the future.

That took toughness, all right. But in a way, that had always been in him. His great problem in the past had been uncertainty as to what he wanted to do, and where he wanted to go.

Now he knew. First, away into space with Renfrew and Blake. And he would spend his time really learning what the science score was.

Three months—more or less—for that.

Then, back here, and over to Dan Magoelson's house —and off, running. Would he reenter the Palace of Immortality immediately? That decision could wait.

It was a curious three months that followed. For a while Caxton felt a sense of awe at the vastness of the cosmos. Silent planets swung into their viewing plates, and faded into remoteness behind them, leaving nostalgic memories of uninhabited, wind-lashed forests and plains, deserted, swollen seas, and nameless suns.

The sight and the remembrance brought loneliness like an ache, and the knowledge, the slow knowledge, that this journeying was not lifting the weight of strangeness that had settled upon them ever since their arrival at Alpha Centauri.

There was nothing here for their souls to feed on, nothing that would satisfactorily fill one year of their lives, let alone fifty. People really do belong to their own era, Caxton thought. He intended to fight that feeling in himself.

But he watched the realization grow on Blake, and he waited for a sign from Renfrew that he felt it, too. The sign didn't come. Then he grew aware of something else: Renfrew was watching him. Watching Blake also, with a hint in his manner of secret knowledge, a suggestion of secret purpose. *We've got to remember he's sick,* Caxton thought. In spite of that warning to himself, Renfrew's perpetual cheerfulness lulled him. Caxton was lying on his bunk at the end of the third month, thinking uneasily about the whole unsatisfactory situation, when the door opened and Renfrew came in.

He carried a paralyzer gun and a rope. He pointed the gun at Caxton and said, "Sorry, Peter. Cassellahat told me to take no chances, so just lie quietly while I tie you up."

"Blake!" Caxton yelled.

Renfrew shook his head gently. "No use," he said. "I was in his room first."

The gun was steady in his fingers, his blue eyes were steely. All Caxton could do was tense his muscles against the ropes as Renfrew tied him, and trust to his belief that he was probably stronger than the other.

Renfrew stepped back finally, said again, "Sorry, Peter." He added, "I hate to tell you this, but both of you went off the deep end mentally when we arrived at Centaurus—you with your Lakeside obsession, and Blake so disturbed about our odor. This is the cure prescribed by the psychologist whom Cassellahat consulted. You're supposed to get a shock as big as the one that knocked you for a loop."

The first time, Caxton paid no attention to the mention of Cassellahat's name. But the second reference snatched his attention. "Oh, come on, now, Jim," he urged, "think hard. That isn't exactly what Cassellahat said. Think. What were the exact words?"

The question seemed to catch at the other man's mind. He stopped. For just a moment he seemed to be trying to remember. The moment went by. He shook himself. He said, "It won't be long now. We're already entering the field of the bachelor sun."

"Bachelor sun!" Caxton shouted.

Renfrew made no reply. The instant the door closed behind him, Caxton began to work on his bonds; all the time he was thinking: What was it Cassellahat had said? Bachelor suns maintained themselves in this space by a precarious balancing.

In this space! The sweat poured down his face as he pictured their vessel being precipitated into another plane of the space-time continuum. He could feel the ship falling as he finally worked his hands free of the rope.

He hadn't been tied long enough for the cords to interfere with his circulation. He headed for Blake's room.

In two minutes, they were on their way to the control room.

Renfrew didn't see them until they had him. Blake grabbed his gun; Caxton hauled him out of the control chair with one mighty heave, and dumped him onto the floor.

He lay there, unresisting, grinning up at them. "Too late," he taunted. "We're approaching the first point of intolerance, and there's nothing you can do except prepare for the shock."

Caxton scarcely heard him. He plumped himself into the chair and glared into the viewing plate. Nothing showed. That stumped him for a second. Then he saw the recorder instruments. They were trembling furiously, registering a body of infinite size.

For a long moment, Caxton stared crazily at those incredible figures. Then he plunged the decelerator far over. Before that pressure of full-driven adeledicnander, the machine grew rigid; Caxton had a sudden fantastic picture of two irresistible forces in full collision. Gasping, he jerked the power out of gear.

They were still falling.

"An orbit," Blake was saying. "Get us into an orbit."

With shaking fingers, Caxton pounded one out on the keyboard, basing his figures on a sun of Sol-ish size, gravity, and mass.

The bachelor wouldn't let them have it.

He tried another orbit, and a third, and more—finally one that would have given them an orbit around mighty Antares itself. But the deadly reality remained. The ship plunged on, down and down.

And there was nothing visible on the plates, not a shadow of substance. It seemed to Caxton that he could make out a vague blur of greater darkness against the black reaches of space. But the stars were few in every direction and it was impossible to be sure.

Finally, in despair, Caxton whirled out of the seat and knelt beside Renfrew, who was still making no effort to get up. "Listen, Jim," he pleaded, "what did you do this for? What's going to happen?"

Renfrew was smiling easily. "Think," he said, "of an old, crusty, human bachelor. He maintains a relationship with his fellows, but the association is as remote as that which exists between a bachelor sun and the stars in the galaxy of which it is a part."

He added, "Any second now, we'll strike the first period of intolerance. It works in jumps like quanta, each period being four hundred and ninety-eight years, seven months and eight days plus a few hours." He grinned. "That's what Cassellahat told me."

It sounded like gibberish. "But what's going to happen?" Caxton urged. "For heaven's sake, man!"

Renfrew gazed up at him blandly; and, looking down at him, Caxton had the sudden, wondering realization that he was sane, the old, completely rational Jim Renfrew, made better somehow, stronger. Renfrew said quietly:

"Why, it'll just knock us out of its toleration area; and in doing so will put us back—"

Jerk!

The lurch was immensely violent. With a bang, Caxton struck the floor, skidded, and then a hand—Renfrew's—caught him. And it was all over.

He stood up, conscious that they were no longer falling. He looked at the instrument board. All the lights were dim, untroubled, the needles firmly at zero. Caxton turned and stared at Renfrew, and at Blake, who was ruefully picking himself up from the floor.

Renfrew said persuasively, "Let me at the control board, Peter. Our ship is probably damaged by all that maneuvering you tried, but I'd like to get near Earth before we have to get into our lifeboat. You two get into your spacesuits, and bring me mine. Hurry. I don't dare accelerate until we're properly dressed."

For a long minute, Caxton looked at him; and then he nodded. Later, he stood by Blake as Renfrew set the controls and pulled the accelerator over. Renfrew looked up.

"We'll reach Earth in about eight hours," he said, "and it'll be about a year and a half after we left five hundred years ago."

A tremendous understanding suddenly flowed in upon Caxton. . . . The bachelor sun, he thought dazedly. In easing them out of its field of toleration, it had simply precipitated them into a period of time beyond its field. Renfrew had said that it worked in jumps of four hundred ninety-eight years and some seven months and—

As Caxton had these awarenesses, the terror of the crisis lifted even more. And the truth of his new situation moved in upon him. He stood there, gripped by an awful realization: *But this means . . . we're back!*

Back in the twentieth century.

And this time, he had only one faint possibility of ever finding the trail to the future again: That movie projector!

XXVI

CAXTON GLARED down at the name in the book of records in the Kissling city hall: Magoelson, Daniel Magoelson. After a while, he unglued his gaze from the page, and he thought of how people were really stereotyped. Magoelson probably used that same name in all the time-periods he went to, presumably trusting that nobody would ever follow him, or trace him.

Normally, who *could* follow him? The other dwellers in the Palace of Immortality! Yes, of course. But they were few in number. And the Possessors evidently considered that the use of one name was a simplification; it undoubtedly prevented confusion. If you were always Daniel Magoelson, then you wouldn't suddenly wonder who you were now. Wherever now happened to be at any given moment.

What bothered Caxton was that it looked as if this was the end of the trail. As he visualized it, a Possessor had temporarily operated a business in Kissling. While there, he had sold Quik-Photo the movie projector that, long ago now, had started this whole mad quest. And then he had gone out of that business, and pretended to move—where? The West Coast; so his earlier inquiries had established.

Even then, Caxton recalled, the move had sounded vague. As he came out onto the street of the little town, Caxton was also recalling that he had actually heard the man's name at the time of that inquiry; only it had seemed unimportant, and had slipped his mind; there were so many names, and so many people, that he had met when he was a salesman for Quik-Photo. Looking back, it seemed like one big blur of nobodies.

Nevertheless, because he was stubborn and refused to make assumptions, he went to the post office and asked if there was a forwarding address for Magoelson. The man who had come to the counter went off somewhere from the little wicket, and presently came back with a card.

"Yes," he said, "we've kept it over the normal time for such things." He explained, "In a little place like this we're simply more obliging, you know."

He was a bald-headed nobody to Caxton, and he would be in his grave one of these days with no choice of living forever; undoubtedly without even a thought about it. But when Caxton put his hand out to take the card, the man drew it back; and he said, "Sorry, I can't show you this. Against the rules. What I can do is take a letter you write and forward it for you. If Mr. Magoelson wants to correspond with you, that's his business." He smiled apologetically.

"Just a moment," said Caxton. "Don't go away."

He walked over behind a pillar, took out his billfold, removed a hundred-dollar bill, which he palmed in such a way that the amount showed. Then he walked back to the wicket and showed the man the bill.

The puffy eyes widened a little. Then the man said in a low voice, "Where can I meet you after four—after work?"

"In the Kissling Hotel," said Caxton.

His palm closed down on the bill. If any portion of the little byplay was witnessed by other clerks, or by the man who had taken up a position behind Caxton, it was not possible for anyone else to have actually seen the money.

Caxton turned away, tense, but with suppressed excitement. It was only a few minutes after noon; so he had a long time to wait.

The hundred-dollar bill price tag on the address meant nothing. After persuading Blake and Renfrew to drop him at his home city, he had gone to a bank where he had left money in a small account, and had written a counter-check. From there he had gone to where he had stored his effects, and from them secured a safety deposit box key. Back to another bank—where the box was under an assumed name—and what a relief when, in the privacy of a little booth, he had lifted the lid of the box and found himself gazing down at the hundred thousand dollars that Renfrew had given him before they departed for Centaurus.

What a relief, yes, and what a validation of his own intent then. The money, of course, had been intended by Renfrew for distribution to creditors and heirs of Peter Caxton. But *he*, with his plan to return, had thought with passionate determination that he would be coming back. And, by God, he had.

Thinking about that moment as he sat in the Kissling Hotel, looking out of the big window onto that drab twentieth century street, Caxton waited for the postal clerk, and thought: *All right, so it was a disaster to be suddenly precipitated by the bachelor sun back to where I started from . . . that was for certain.*

But surely the money being there, waiting for him just as he had envisioned it, surely this was an omen that everything that had happened was not in vain.

The feeling of coming victory grew stronger when,

about eight minutes after four, the clerk walked into the hotel and the two men went outside and down a side street, where the money was exchanged for a little white card with an address on it.

"I copied it," said the clerk, "from the one on file." He added, "You won't tell him where you got it?"

"No, of course not." Over his shoulder as he turned away, Caxton added, "Perfectly understood."

He had already glanced at the address. It was in Lakeside; not the West Coast at all. Pretty tricky.

It was dark when he arrived at the small Kissling airport shortly after nine that night. He paid the taxi driver, and was only dimly aware at first of the man who walked up past the car and followed him closely.

Too closely. Caxton turned.

As he did so, a gloved hand grabbed his left elbow with a hard grip. Caxton had a fleeting glimpse of the face of Kameel Bustaman, and he thought he heard Bustaman say, "I'm sorry, Peter, but you're too dangerous a man for me to have around. . . ."

XXVII

THE YEAR WAS 2026 A.D., and though the computer-controlled projector at Tichenor Collegiate was aware in an electronic sense that something was wrong, it continued functioning.

Similarly, the film distribution machine that operated from the nearby big city was also aware of an error. But the disturbance was not the kind that triggered its decision-making mechanism into action. Not at first, anyway. Not in time.

An order came through from Tichenor by the usual electronic channels. The order was of human origin. First, the number of the film was punched, then the assigned number of the school. Usually, when the film was in its place in the library, no other human agency was required. However, if the film and all its duplicates were out on loan, a red light flashed in the projection room at Tichenor, and then it was up to the would-be renter to order a substitute film.

On this occasion a copy of the film was available. The electronic imprint of the number of the school was stamped onto the container's sensitives, and onto a series of bookkeeping plates. The bookkeeping plates moved through a machine which took information from them, as a result of which money was collected from Tichenor in due time. The film flashed out of its shelf into a tube.

Its speed at the beginning was not great. Instant by instant other film containers clicked into the tube in front of it or behind it, and constant automatic readjustments of speed were necessary to prevent collisions. The number of *the* film's destination, Tichenor Collegiate, was 9-7-43-6-2—Zone 9, Main Tube 7, Suburban Tube 43, Distribution 6, School 2.

The cutoff at Zone 9 opened in its automatic fashion as the forces from the film container activated the mechanism. A moment later, the film was in main mail channel number 7. It was the channel of small packages, and they were strung out in an endless train, each in its electronically controlled container. The train never stopped, but it slowed and speeded as new containers were precipitated into the tube, or old ones darted away into cutoffs to their separate destinations.

43-6-2. With a click, the film arrived in the receptor. Automatic devices slipped it into position on the projector and, at a set time—in this case about an hour later—the projector's seeing eye attachment opened and surveyed the auditorium. Several students were still in the aisles. It clanged a warning alarm, waited a half minute, then locked the auditorium doors, and once more slid the cover from its eye. This time a single student remained in the aisle.

The projector clanged its final alarm for the students. The next warning would be a light flash in the principal's office, together with a television picture of the auditorium, which would clearly show the recalcitrant student. This final action proved unnecessary. The youth, an individual named Kameel Bustaman, ceased his capering and tumbled into a seat. The showing began.

It was not within the capacity of the electronic devices of the projector to realize that young Bustaman was an unknowing Possessor who could have a time-changing influence on one or more objects around him. The effect—as Johns had discovered—was always random, but it usually fixed on one thing. In this instance, the proper film showed on the screen, but the film that was subsequently put into the container and returned to the film library was an obsolete creation called "Food Magic," lent to Tichenor Collegiate by the Arlay Film Library in 1979.

All of the subsequent "work" done in 1979 by Claudan Johns and Selanie operating out of the trailer on Piffer's Road, and by the Possessor Daniel Magoelson, who sold a special movie projector to Quik-Photo (who sold it to Tichenor), was designed to take advantage of this accidental but unavoidable time influence so near the lower end of the backfold in time—only two years from 1977. Their hope was that the imbalance created (properly utilized) would enable them to locate the timefold when it again moved forward.

On the other hand, Bustaman's interference with their efforts was based on a suspicion that what they were doing was somehow aimed at him. No amount of reassurance from the Possessors could alleviate that abysmal suspicion.

By pure chance, none of the containers which subsequently acquired a 1979 film went out on call until it was too late. When one finally clicked into position on another projector and began to roll, Caxton had dismantled the 1979 projector, and the sequential process of time connection had been broken.

Bustaman brought Caxton, bound hand and foot, to November 14, 9812 A.D.—the last day of time. Twelve minutes and a few seconds remained of the known universe. It was 7:59 P.M., and the end was due at 8:11 P.M. plus thirty-one seconds.

These facts Bustaman explained to his prisoner in an even voice, and finished, "In twelve minutes, Peter, you're going over the edge."

Caxton stared dully up at his captor. He had been conscious long enough to sink into a hopeless state. And so he merely said, not sharply, not with any real interest, "Why would you consider me dangerous?"

"You've got all that accumulation of time energy in your cells, that's why."

The thought crossed Caxton's mind that, if that was the real problem, why hadn't Bustaman simply killed him? Why this bizarre fate? Since it was a possibility that must surely have occurred to the older man, he asked the question aloud.

Bustaman was surprised. "I guess you don't understand your situation, Peter. You've got more time energy accumulated in your cells than any other person who ever lived. Nobody knows what would happen to the surrounding environment if you were suddenly shot. And, of course, if the Possessors ever got hold of you now with all that energy, they might feel motivated to train your special ability. But even if they didn't, sooner or later you would create an excessive disturbance in time—and that's something which I, with my purposes, cannot allow. So that's the picture. Believe me, I don't know anywhere else to put that much time energy except over the edge." He broke off. "It's like the problem they used to have with radioactive materials before they were able to shoot them off into the sun. I'm discharging you into the only equivalent of the sun that I know of."

As he gazed into those flinty eyes, and saw in them

no mercy, Caxton shivered. And then he said in a trembling voice, "Claudan Johns didn't seem to think back in the seventeenth century that I had any extra ability."

"That's because the probabilities you had been put into in the Palace didn't take. So there was nowhere for you to go. But now you've got more than twice as much energy."

"But why not help me? Maybe we could work together. You found me willing before."

"I'm sorry, Peter. In such a partnership, I'd soon be the lesser. I could never trust a paranoid."

The two paranoids gazed at each other, and then Bustaman glanced at his watch. "Five minutes to go," he said. "The timing on the world's end was worked out by Claudan on a comparison basis from inside the Palace. I don't care to trust it to the exact second, though he's pretty good at such things. But I'm taking no chances. I'm leaving right now."

He hastily removed the timepiece from his wrist, and laid it on the floor beside Caxton. "Here. This will give you something to do."

With equal haste, he headed for an open door ten feet away and went through it.

A moment later, he came charging back in. He was pale. "For God's sake, what have you done to me? I can't move through time any more. I've lost my Possessor ability."

He had a key in his hand. He knelt beside Caxton and, fingers shaking, unlocked something in the chains that bound Caxton. Hastily he got up, drawing the chain clear. He backed swiftly to the center of the room and stood there, mumbling, "Bringing you all the way up here . . . I was with you too long. . . . Oh, my God, we're both doomed."

The man's terror suddenly made the threat more real. Caxton stood up on watery legs. And yet, after a moment, he was stronger. The other man's face, once so hard and determined, had taken on a pasty complexion; and somehow that braced him. He had a vagrant thought: *Maybe the big, tough sales managers aren't really so tough after all.*

The thought ended. For, just like that, Bustaman was beside him, clutching at his arm. "Peter, listen," he moaned, "after I took you from the hotel roof, I decided to use you two ways. One to take care of Johns. The other—I split off a probability of you and transported it into the Palace, where I have a hydrogen bomb. I was going to use your knowledge to help me blow up the Palace of Immortality and all those bastards." He gulped, then rushed on, "Look, there's a way you can take me there—the way Johns was able to take along that trailer and the way I was able to bring you up here. Quick, here's what you do—"

Caxton said, "Am I tied up . . . back there?" One look into that stricken, guilty face told him that he had guessed a grim truth. He muttered, "You were going to go from here to where that bomb is, and force me to explode it?"

After a moment, the mere remark seemed like an inadequate reaction. With every ounce of his strength, he struck his fist into Bustaman's face. The agony of the blow flashed all the way along his arm to his shoulder, surging into the first racing steps of a hundred-yard dash, he pushed at Bustaman. They both fell hard. Caxton's breath was knocked out of him, and so he lay there on top of his enemy, breathing gaspingly; and he had a wondering thought:

I'll be damned. Petie Caxton turns out to be a good guy after all, for heaven's sake!

They had fallen beside Bustaman's watch. And, as Caxton had that exhilarating, glorious realization about himself, he glimpsed the face of the timepiece. The time was 8:11 plus—as he glared at it—thirty-one seconds. . . .

XXVIII

CAXTON HAD a dream then. A voice said, "All right, tune him through—"

The next instant—

He was walking into the Kissling airport. It was as he pushed through the revolving door that his first fleeting memory came.

He involuntarily stopped. Or, rather, he tried to stop. The door propelled him forward from the night outside into the bright interior. Several people brushed past him. It was a narrow place, and Caxton was at the counter and handing his bag to the attendant before he was able to remember again.

The recollection seemed a little vaguer now.

"You'll have to hurry, sir," the clerk's voice came through to him. "The plane leaves in four minutes. Better just carry your bag."

So there he was running along a corridor and out across a stretch of concrete to the plane. Up the escalator and into the machine, last one aboard, breathless.

Where did the time go? I thought I was in plenty of time.

The door wheezed shut behind him. A brief conversation with the stewardess, and then into a seat beside a man who tried to sell him insurance.

And every minute, what had happened seemed further away, yet not untrue, as if it were something at a distance in his past.

Shortly after ten the next morning, Caxton turned in at the gate of the address in Lakeside, where Daniel Magoelson lived. As he made his way to the door, he saw that it was an elegant mansion on a large lot. At the door he paused. For long moments, then, he stood there, Peter Caxton, filled with his purposes, stiffening himself for the confrontation, a man who had, as a person, almost nothing but his subjectiveness to offer any situation; but who never ceased trying to force to where he wanted to be.

Trouble-maker, determined lover, creative in his specialty, a destroyer in most other situations. Wherever he was there was some kind of turmoil that, traced back, turned out to have been caused by him.

But he was alive, and he had his right to his three score and ten—or more if he could get it. He was charming with women, and quite a few had loved him, mistaking his selfishness for firmness of character.

The door was opening.

XXIX

INSTANTS LATER, the man who stood enframed in the doorway said, "Yes, I am Dan Magoelson." Oddly, Caxton had no immediate reaction. He was noticing that Magoelson was tall, friendly of manner, and at ease. The Possessor looked to be about thirty years old.

It was that neutral, the first contact, and *that* rigid. Caxton parted his lips to speak his prepared opening lines: "Magoelson, I've been following you for thirteen hundred years—" He never said them, for Magoelson spoke first.

"Come in, Peter," he said, "but please excuse me if I don't let you too close." The Possessor smiled. "All that time energy needs to be not less than four, preferably six, feet away from a Possessor, you'll agree."

The words, with their instant understanding of the danger he represented, brought Caxton the sudden fear that at this twelfth hour he might still lose. He poised there, slightly bent forward as if to walk, yet not daring to say anything, or move.

Magoelson continued, "We've been expecting you. Your friends are here."

That reached through the intense caution. "My— friends?" Caxton echoed. And then, again, he froze. In his taut state the meaning of that was . . . blank. He could not imagine friends. He was a lifetime loner. He had nobody he called by the name of friend.

231

Magoelson had stepped back. He beckoned. Automatically, Caxton walked forward into the hallway, and, at the other man's gesture, moved on almost timidly to the entrance of a large living room. There he came to a teetering halt.

He stood there. He stared. He tried to speak, but no words would come. Finally Renfrew and Blake must have realized that the shock was too great, and they hurried over in alarm and both said something like, "Peter, take it easy. Easy does it."

The first distant, conscious thought that came to Caxton was that he was in the position of the amateur criminal who has been caught red-handed at the scene of the crime. Through his mind flashed a kaleidoscope of all of his secret actions and the lies that he had initiated in his relationship with those two men.

And stronger than before was the reaction: too much. . . . He was the outwardly respectable banker of a small town caught in a criminal act, and it was too much. . . .

Caxton stood there, and the tears started to his eyes and ran down his cheeks. Then he stumbled over to a couch, dimly aware that Blake and Renfrew were assisting him. But their help made no difference. The tears flowed unchecked.

Too much. Five hundred years to Centaurus in a cataleptic state, then over eight hundred years from the seventeenth century up, again, to 2476 A.D., a frozen body. And now, this abrupt exposure. . . . For God's sake, how much can a human being stand?

Somewhere in there, shame came. And because tears do stop, and muscle spasms of grief can eventually be controlled, there came a moment when he took out his handkerchief and blew his nose, and dried his face; and this time when he looked up he was able to see that the other three men were sitting watching him without judgment.

Blake shook his head as Caxton's eyes met his, and said, "We're with you, pal." Renfrew's blue, blue eyes were slightly misted. "I guess there're two sentimentalists here, my dear friend," he said.

Magoelson, who was still looking neutral, leaned forward and said, "I've been telling Mr. Blake and Mr. Renfrew of your last travail."

Caxton waited. He assumed at once that the reference was to his time journey from 1653 A.D., and he was about to say something that would take that knowledge for granted, when the hopeful thought occurred: *Maybe they* don't *know!*

If they didn't, he was certainly not going to tell them.

Blake stood up and came over, and stood smiling down at him, shaking his head chidingly. "If confession is good for the soul, Peter, you'll never know that goodness." He went on. "Look, my friend, we know the main facts."

And as Caxton listened, astonished, Blake proceeded to give him a brief account of Caxton's first Palace of Immortality experience, and then of the seventeenth century episode and its aftermath. And then he described how, as Renfrew and he had landed at one of the Renfrew estates, a Possessor had come aboard and persuaded them not to reveal to the world the return of the time travelers.

He had explained to them that mechanical sensors had spotted the presence of a ship from another time. "They couldn't," Blake added, "get to us before we dropped you off, but they managed to head us off."

And, of course, as soon as Renfrew and he had understood that even the lifeboat was big enough to create another probability world, dangerous here so close to 1977, well—

Blake broke off at that point and concluded, "Peter, I've got to hand it to you. The way you faced me in the hotel up there in 2476 after all you'd been through was a masterpiece of deception. But you can stop all that, and remember that the main body of Possessors are good hearted people; so there's a complete solution for all of us." He turned to the single Possessor in the room. "Tell him, Mr. Magoelson."

Magoelson stood up slowly. He was smiling again. "Yes, Peter, you've won—let me qualify that—as much as you can win, which we hope and believe will satisfy you."

Swiftly, he made the series of statements that clarified his meaning:

For Blake and Renfrew acceptance by, and admission to, the Palace of Immortality. They were both, it seemed, the type of individual (although not themselves Possessors) who fitted completely into the requirements for new members.

"Eventually in our work," said Magoelson, "we would have found them and enlisted them anyway. As it is, we were delighted that they qualified, and so we are able to pay a satisfactory price for their cooperation. Now, you, Peter—"

It appeared that for Caxton there could not be total acceptance ". . . for reasons which have been previously explained to you."

But he would be allowed periodic admission, so that he could reverse his age and maintain himself forever.

Magoelson continued, "You'll be wanting some evidence that this is all in good faith." He waved at the big room. "What do you think of this house?" he asked.

Caxton did not look around, did not move. What was coming, he had no idea. But he was beginning to recover from his breakdown, and beginning to remember his purpose in searching for this house. What was happening here—what he hoped to accomplish—*was absolutely necessary.* So he was not about to commit himself. "It seems to be the home of a well-to-do person," he said in an even tone.

"It's the entrance in this era to the Palace of Immortality," was the reply, "and this is where you will be living for the next few years while you learn the ropes."

Again the smile, but the tall man's lean face was oddly tense. "What do you think?" the man asked. He finished almost apologetically, "This is the best the other Possessors will let me do for you, Peter."

Caxton grew aware that all three men were watching him anxiously. Startling, that . . . *So Renfrew and Blake have been told that I'm considered one of the twenty percent of males in this half century who are paranoid,* he thought. He felt momentarily degraded by the realization that they knew. It braced him to say what he had to. "I don't really understand the restriction," he said. He explained, "In one of my lucid moments, I took a look at this whole probability complex; and so my question is, why don't you just merge me with the grown-up version of the fourteen-year-old Caxton that Price said you Possessors would contact and split off?"

"It hasn't been done yet."

He could have let that be the answer. If it was true, he had nothing to fear. Yet he realized that his impulse was to tell them his whole scheme, in essence. And find out right now if they could stop him.

If they could, he had better settle for what they offered.

Aloud, stubbornly, he said, "I can't see that making any difference."

Magoelson said, "We'll merge you as soon as Claudan Johns in his own good time releases the method for going earlier than 1977. Don't forget you were fourteen—when? Before 1977, right?"

"Makes no difference," persisted Caxton. "That Peter Caxton was contacted at a future time you and I may not know about. But starting at an age prior to his fourteen, he's been existing in his own probability. And so he's around somewhere. Isn't that so?"

Magoelson smiled his gentle smile. "True. But"—he shook his head—"that only means that somewhere in the future a Possessor knows what probability world that Peter Caxton is in, and where it is."

However, he went on, here and now nobody knew. "But we agree," said Magoelson, "that very likely *all* of your potential probabilities are in existence. But we cannot contact them for you."

It was still a lack of understanding. "Listen," said Caxton flatly, "it's all got to have happened already. In a universe of endless probabilities, they've already merged. So why doesn't that totally merged Peter Caxton up there somewhere"—he waved vaguely toward the north—"come back here and dissolve my paranoia?"

Magoelson's smile was suddenly grim. "Yes," he said, "why haven't you?" He did not wait for Caxton to reply. He continued earnestly, "Your question is one reason why Claudan Johns remains such a stubborn experimenter. He has asked the same question."

"Is that your best answer?" Caxton asked.

"I can't imagine a better one," was the reply.

Caxton said no more. His hope *had to be* that the non-participating experimenter, Johns, and the good-hearted Possessors had indeed failed to analyze what seemed so obvious to a paranoid.

He grew aware that Magoelson had turned away from him, toward Renfrew and Blake. "All right, gentlemen," he said. The two men stood up. Magoelson glanced over his shoulder at Caxton. "I'm taking them into the Palace," he explained. "They'll be back in a few days. And in and out regularly from now on." He drew a keyring out of his pocket and placed it on the table beside the door. "These are for the outer door, and for the west-wing apartment"—he gestured—"which we are assigning to be your private quarters."

Caxton walked over to the table and took the keys. Entrance to this building, he had analyzed, was one of three preliminaries to action that he absolutely had to have in his control. Then he went with the trio up to the second floor and into the room where one wall was strangely misty. Through it he could see the giant stairway. He shook hands with his friends and with Magoelson, and, as he watched them go through the fog and up the steps, he was thinking: *So they don't really know after 1653 A.D. They don't know about Bustaman and me up there at 9812.*

Idly, mind almost blank, he watched as the three men made it to the huge doors of the Palace of Immortality, opened one of them and went through it. When they were gone out of sight, and when the door had closed behind him, Caxton turned away, and thought: *This is the victory they're willing for me to have.*

He tasted it with his mind, and found it flat and unappetizing.

He explored the house, and it was all there, as beautiful inside as it had been outside. The west wing was a lovely, self-contained apartment; he presently made himself some lunch there and sat in the kitchen breakfast nook with a book from 2863 A.D. propped up before him.

The English in which it was printed was exactly the same as twentieth century American. So it must be from a probability world where *that* had been maintained. The book was a novel, and it showed human beings in a sexually free society where every woman slept with every man who wanted her provided she could fit him into her schedule. And, if she couldn't—if she just didn't have the time—the man understood perfectly, and was not mad about it because his schedule was pretty tight, also. Except for the more universal lovingness, people did much the same thing as Caxton had always done. They ate, they worked, they studied, they slept, they played games.

This is victory. This is what I shall have. This is what I fought for.

Victory, that is, if he accepted their offer.

It was not totally nothing, because he did like to read; always had. And so he read that novel all the way through. And then he read a second one in which the problem was that a beautiful, desirable girl got injured without anyone, including herself, knowing it. She began to reject all her lovers, and soon went into seclusion to think about life and its true meaning. In the end, the injury was discovered. Medical science rushed in to cure her, and soon she was back with her boyfriends, smiling through tears of regret at the trouble she had caused, and living a normal existence again.

Caxton presumed that the background described was but one probability, and that others of the twenty-ninth century would show a different interrelation of people.

But how many basic switches could there be?

It was minutes after midnight as he had that negative consideration, and put away the second book. But, as he undressed, he nevertheless reaffirmed to himself: *Okay. So it may all be just repetition. But it's better to be alive and doing the same things than to be dead and doing nothing.*

He got into bed. Then set the alarm on a peculiar but recognizable bedside clock to wake him at about half past the third wee hour.

It was decision.

It was rejection of the small offer made by the Possessors.

Afterwards, he lay wide awake, thinking: *Kind of ridiculous if now I can't sleep. . . .*

He wakened to a sound: the alarm, a series of small bell-like tings.

The clock showed 3:42 A.M. A good time for the beginning . . . *Let me*, he thought, *call this the moment.* He spoke the next words aloud: "My whole future shall be computed from 3:42 A.M., August 10, 1981."

Obvious that for the Big Thought of all time and space, there had to be an exact moment from which there was no turning back.

"Okay." He projected the action words aloud also. "All right, you Peter Caxton out there. Start merging me."

XXX

At 10:28 the next morning, Peter Caxton sat in the west-wing apartment kitchen eating breakfast. The sound of a door opening came from behind him.

Without turning, he said, "Good morning, Mr. Johns." Silence.

He's thinking about the implications of my knowing who he is, Caxton thought, smugly.

Aloud, still without turning, he said, "I've got a plate here for you. Why don't you join me?"

No answer.

"You may be interested to know," Caxton continued, "that I assumed the truth of your statements, accepted literally that past time waits forever. Future time, also, of course."

He brought up one arm and hand. And waved vaguely to take in the horizon. "I assumed I was out there in every time dimension, every era between now and 9812 A.D., multiplied, well"—he paused tolerantly—"since each one would somewhere take time to accomplish, and would eventually have to be created by an effort—and more important—I'd have to keep records of where they all were, I limited the number to one hundred.

"So I imagine," went on Caxton, casually, "one of these centuries, I'll start building the Palace of Immortality. You may ask, did I really build it? And my answer is, who else could it be—or will it be?"

Still no sound from the person who had opened the rear door and come into the apartment. Suddenly, that was slightly irritating to Caxton. His voice had an edge in it, as he said, "The question arises, can anyone stop me now? As far as I can reason it, the answer is no. Any comments?"

Since there was again no reply, he had his first tiny doubt. . . . *After all,* he thought, *it is hard to keep track. So maybe I've got it mixed.*

Maybe it isn't Johns.

Whereupon, he turned in his chair, intending to look . . .

Caxton awakened to the sound of Selanie's laughter. He opened his eyes and looked up at the trailer ceiling. When the man's voice came gaspingly, Caxton wondered what was going on. He assumed the man was her father, because who else would it be on this second day after their arrival into 1653 A.D.?

What was puzzling about the voice was that the man seemed to be gasping for breath. And once, in that gasping way, he said, "Let up, Selanie. That's enough for a first time."

"No, sir," came the girl's voice, "forty minutes." And she laughed again, gaily.

It sort of sounded like fun, and it was incredibly mysterious. Caxton dressed hurriedly and made his way outside. He came upon an unexpected sight.

Johns, stripped to the waist, was running slowly past the door of the trailer. The girl ran beside him, and once, when he faltered, she caught him and pulled him along. The two disappeared around the front of the trailer and Caxton could hear their feet thudding down the other side. They presently reappeared around the rear. The girl saw Caxton and called out cheerfully, "Join us, Mr. Caxton!"

The idea was too ludicrous for Caxton, who had almost literally never exercised in his life. He shook his head.

Father and daughter ran around the trailer twice as he stood there. *I suppose I ought to go and shave and make myself presentable,* Caxton thought. But he glanced speculatively at the sun, which was surprisingly high in the heavens. About nine o'clock, he guessed, or even later.

He climbed the hill and looked out over the same empty miles that he remembered from the other probability. *This is real,* he thought. *Because I'm here without knowing how I came, or who that person was at the door, in the Magoelson house.* He looked down at the trailer, and at the two people who were slowly—the man awkwardly—running around it still. And then once more he surveyed the distant horizons of the timeless day; and the reality grew grimmer.

These probabilities are really solid, he thought.

He walked down the hill, uncertain. The other mergings had seemed as if they were under the control of a Peter Caxton somewhere. But this one was a mystery.

He did notice that he had no impulse toward his nervous breakdown response to anxiety. So that was a change.

Ignoring the father and daughter, he entered the trailer, located the toilet, relieved himself, and then searched for and found the same kind of shave salve as he had used on his first visit to the Palace of Immortality. As then, it was a case of rub on the salve, then rub off the beard. Next he used his pocket comb to straighten his hair. Feeling fairly presentable, he went outdoors a second time and sat down to wait out the jogging session.

Caxton watched the two people with narrowed, appraising eyes. He realized that his evaluation of the girl could not avoid awareness of her attractiveness as a sexual being; yet he now saw that her face, though that of a nineteen-year-old in many respects—the clearness of the skin, the youthfulness of it—still had other, more mature characteristics. Without fixing on any number, he wondered how old she was in terms of years. Several times, as she ran past, she glanced at him with eyes that appraised *him* in a totally ungirlish fashion. And when the morning's run was finally over, the father and daughter came to where he sat and the daughter said:

"I discovered last night that the glove damaged Father more than I had at first realized. His whole body suffered an energy loss; suddenly he was maintaining his self-esteem with the peculiar mystical idea that he was a person especially loved by God."

From somewhere, Caxton had an instant understanding of the condition. "Oh," he said. "Oh, that." Even as he spoke, he dismissed his interest in the matter, unwilling to probe into the dream-like world of merging memories. Why had he been merged back here without warning? That was what he had to put his attention on.

The girl was looking at him with an odd expression. "Mr. Caxton, Father and I have been discussing this situation, and since he seems to be in a weakened condition—though he's already better—it looks like you're going to have to be the man of this expedition. If you're willing, I'm prepared to play my role"—she smiled in a friendly fashion—"a sort of man and wife relation, wouldn't you say?"

Afterward, Caxton could never quite remember all the emotions that moved through him as he realized the meaning of Selanie's words. There was outrage that in this second probability the relationship which he had craved in the first one would be easy. And her suggestion, if you please.

Part of the outrage came from the realization that apparently his degraded cells meant nothing under these circumstances. The time odor was dismissed this time as if it was of no importance. The reason for it was an angle he had not realized on the first go-round: a woman's need for security, satisfied *then*, of course, by the real father. And so no substitutes had been needed, thank you. By God!

The passion of that faded also. A faint regret remained that he would probably not be able to remain and take advantage of the offer.

She must have noticed his hesitation, for she said, "Of course, if you're not interested . . ." She turned away.

"Wait!" Caxton said urgently. "I want to tell you both the truth of this situation."

The girl faced him again. The old man stared at Caxton with interest.

Caxton told them what had happened to him.

He did not mention how they had escaped from the other probability. That had to be his hold on them, in case he needed leverage.

Claudan Johns said, "I deduce now that the glove Bustaman gave you was more heavily charged than was necessary for what he wanted. As a result, interacted to produce two, perhaps even many, probabilities." His own words seemed to stimulate him. Something of the Johns that Caxton remembered was suddenly visible. "What do you need from us?" he asked shrewdly.

Caxton hesitated, startled by the implication of the question.

What bothered Caxton was the idea that he might still need something. And that this was why he was here. He said slowly, "I think everything necessary is done. I accumulated the time energy. That absolutely had to be the preliminary. Next, I gained access to the Palace. That was necessary. I have now merged with thirty-nine of a hundred postulated Peter Caxtons. The others are out there still, presumably aware right now of what they should be doing, and guarding this whole condition. So"—he shrugged—"I think I'm just collecting the body in this probability." He glanced at the girl. "What do you think?" he said.

There had been a developing troubled expression on her face. At his question, she cheered up. "I think we ought to have breakfast," she said in her brilliant voice. "And if you're still here afterward, we can then discuss your future, and ours."

He was still . . . here . . . afterward.

It had been a silent breakfast. But as they came out of the trailer after eating, Claudan Johns said that he believed he had analyzed the most likely reason for Caxton's return to this seventeenth century probability. "You're here," he said, "to learn my method of going at will earlier than 1977."

Caxton parted his lips to deny the analysis. But he closed them together again without speaking. He would let them believe, he decided, that they had some power in this situation.

What he did finally say aloud was, "What is your price for the method?"

The man and the girl did an astonishingly naïve thing. They looked at each other. Then, as if by mutual consent, Selanie said, "Mr. Caxton, tell us again exactly what you propose to do."

Caxton did not reply immediately.

As he stood there, a squawking bird flew over his head. A breeze blew gently into his face, bringing the scent of greenery and grass and the odor of marsh water. Above was blueness, a whole vast skyful of it, with only here and there a trace of cloud. Wonderful, incredible universe, apparently complete in every detail.

Involuntarily, he found himself staring at the stupendous outer scene of innumerable probability worlds like this. And of the Possessor plan to transform every person who had ever lived into a peaceful type, who would then merge with all other probabilities of himself. And so every human being from the dawn of man would one day be alive forever.

Once more, as he had in the wee hours in the Magoelson house, he thought of it as the most colossally wonderful idea ever conceived.

And he reaffirmed it to be his ideal also. As it was theirs.

His face hardened.

Regardless of consequences, he thought grimly. No one can be allowed to get in the way of such a desirable purpose.

All opposition must be suppressed or brushed forcibly aside.

Stupid people cannot be permitted to interfere.

Those who resist, or seriously hinder, the grand goal will be the only ones who are not recreated into a future probability world. Bustaman, as a starter.

Standing there, he explained to Selanie and her father the beautiful perfection of his ideal. And was startled when the girl shook her head, and said, "Dad, don't give him the secret."

"Huh!" said Caxton. He glared at her. "Are you out of your mind? This is what you want, isn't it?"

She gazed at him earnestly. "No, Mr. Caxton, this is not what we want. You have just done the paranoid perversion of a good idea. And we don't want any part of it."

Even as she spoke, Caxton was recovering. He didn't need their help. Because his theory included the method of going earlier than 1977. So he could afford to be tolerant of the young woman's opposition.

Nonetheless, he felt innocent. *For God's sake,* he thought, *I didn't ask to be a paranoid. It was all automatic. I feel as if I can be reasoned with.*

He said as much to Johns, continuing, "We seem to be divided on the fine point of how the deed shall be done. Millions of paranoids have learned to control their unconscious drive to kill. How can we make certain that I will not revert at some future moment of stress? That would be the problem, would it not, with every paranoid who attains a position of power?"

"No question," replied Johns, "you have stated the problem." He was smiling. "However, since you obviously did create all this, and did build the Palace—"

"Will," corrected Caxton.

There was a look, suddenly, in the older man's eyes. Somehow, he must have missed that thought in what Caxton had previously described to him. "My God"—he almost breathed the words rather than spoke them—"you mean, you haven't done it yet?"

It was the great moment. For this was his magnificent idea. "I haven't done *anything*," said Caxton. He added casually, "Someday, I'll take the time necessary to set up those hundred Peter Caxtons." He broke off. "Meanwhile, I must keep exact records."

Claudan Johns said after a long pause, "Obviously, I must give my secret to the man who solved *that* problem."

Caxton glanced at the girl. She was pale but resigned. She caught his look. "I trust Dad's reasoning," she said in a subdued voice. "On some things he's never wrong."

Just like that, her words brought the dazzling insight. "I've become aware," Caxton said, "of why I'm *really* here."

"You're here to get my father's secret," she replied.

"No, no. I know it." He was impatient. He snatched a notebook from his inside breast pocket, wrote something, tore off the sheet and handed it, folded, to the girl.

To Johns, he said, "What's the secret?"

The old man did not hesitate. "I reasoned that whoever had built this whole time container had left at least one probability way open to the past. It took me a while to find it, but there it eventually was."

Caxton turned to the girl. "Read the note," he said.

She unfolded the paper he had given her and read aloud, "Since I shall sooner or later get around to building all this, I will leave a way open to the past."

"Why not the future, also?" asked Johns, curious.

"That's already done," said Caxton. He explained, "My dream . . . after Bustaman captured me, and we went over the edge of time. There I suddenly was, back at the airport. My guess is that I could merge at any time with the self that went beyond the barrier. But I feel reluctant, cautious. Maybe we all have a dream of what it will be like beyond the barrier. Yet most of us are in no hurry to go." He shrugged. "The job to be done down here is big enough."

"You said," prompted Johns, "that you had just realized why you were here."

Caxton smiled. He felt strangely relaxed. He did not look at the girl as he spoke. "What your daughter just said, that in some things you are never wrong, reminded me that your vast experience as the observer and the experimenter makes you in a manner of speaking the king of the Possessors. The thought has many times been in my mind that sooner or later I must make my peace with you and ensure that I have the benefit of your knowledge. So my purpose to that extent is in character—that is, selfish. But it is a traditional type of selfishness, which I feel may solve all the problems we have discussed."

He finished, simply, "Clearly, I'm here to marry the king's daughter while she is in a predicament where she cannot turn me down."

Having spoken, he glanced at the girl. There was sudden color in her cheeks. So the hormones were still dancing somewhere inside her, he thought happily, despite her real age.

The woman was shaking her head. "What I offered you earlier, Mr. Caxton, was a temporary expedient. But before I make a decision about marriage, I must be in a free condition." She broke off. "How did Dad and I escape from the other seventeenth century probability world?"

The crisis came upon him as swiftly—and naturally—as that. This had to happen without enforcement. Caxton stood there on the grass, blank. Then he gazed uneasily up at that perfect sky. Finally he said, "I guess

I'll have to take that chance, also, won't I?" He sighed. "All right. . . ."

He told them what had happened. Described how that Selanie had merged with the slightly older Selanie that Price had created in the Palace of Immortality.

For a prolonged moment after he finished, the girl stood with a faint smile on her face. Then she said, "Under the circumstances, it would be a little difficult for me to marry you."

"How do you mean?" asked the instantly disappointed Caxton.

"Dad," said the girl, with a quick look at her father, where he stood beside Caxton, "are you doing what you should be doing?"

"I'm doing it," was the enigmatic reply.

She vanished.

Caxton blinked. And she was gone, during that instant.

Caxton swallowed. Then he turned and stared at the old man. There was an edge of bitterness in his voice, as he asked, "Same merge?"

"Same." Laconically. "And now," continued Claudan Johns, "I'd like to merge you with the Peter Caxton up in the Magoelson kitchen."

"But that one merged here," Caxton pointed out.

"Well"—the old man was smiling—"these probability things are a little confusing sometimes. My guess is that, since you believed it was me standing there at the door, in another probability of that scene it *was* me—"

Caxton said, "Oh, for heaven's sake!"

The rugged face, which seemed to be completely back to normal, was smiling still. The eyes were bright. "People who have done this merging a lot tend to protect themselves by utilizing several probabilities. Or else it just happens automatically."

"What are you suggesting?"

"That the you that came down here was undoubtedly the one in the probability where I will be the person at the door. Clearly, you had to come back here first. I was the one who probably merged you back here. And so—"

A great light was dawning. "So that other me is still sitting in the kitchen, still in the act of turning to see who's at the door."

"Correct. And as you turn, I merge this Peter Caxton"—he took his hand out of his pocket, and there was a tiny instrument in it, which he pointed at Caxton—"with that one. And so now, as you turn, you'll suddenly have the memory of this experience. . . ."

. . . Sitting there in the kitchen on that August day in 1981, Caxton looked around. As he saw who was standing at the door, he jumped to his feet.

Selanie walked slowly toward him. She was somewhat older than the girl he had left minutes ago. But it was her great smile that she gave him.

She seemed so friendly, so *warm*, that Caxton said uncertainly, "Your final words were that it would be difficult for you to marry me. I'd like to know why."

She paused. "Think, now," she said.

He didn't know what to think. But again her manner was sensationally . . . open. Something inside Caxton, an almost forgotten something, began to expand.

Selanie said airily, "I can't marry you because the me that I merged with, is already married to you, remember?"

The feeling of something expanding inside him was growing more specific. The actual sensation was as if that other, younger Peter Caxton, the one Price had merged with him long ago (and it didn't take), was suddenly able to move up out of the dark psychic hole where he had been kept until this moment. Able to actually merge with what, until this instant, had been the unremittingly alienated personality of the original Caxton.

The woman concluded, somewhat needlessly, "I'll be living with you here . . . from now on."

EPILOGUE

Señor Pedro del Corteya packed away his projector. He was vaguely unhappy. Poor audience response always affected him that way. It was late when he got outside, but he stood for a moment beside his car looking thoughtfully up at the star-filled night. Blue was that sky above, alive with the mystery of the immense universe. Corteya scarcely noticed. He was thinking: *It's those novelty films that bored them. I have shown too many in this town. No more.*

He began to feel better, as if a weight had lifted from his spirit. He climbed into his car and headed home. As he drove, a voice in his mind said, "All right, tuners, the job is done. Only person we couldn't save was Bustaman. But the barrier held."

The voice ceased, having impressed del Corteya not at all. He was an utterly practical being who paid no attention to the stray thoughts that incessantly muttered their way through his brain.

ACE RECOMMENDS . . .

THE BROKEN LANDS by Fred Saberhagen	08130 — 50¢
THE MOON OF GOMRATH by Alan Garner	53850 — 50¢
MOONDUST by Thomas Burnett Swann	54200 — 50¢
THE SILKIE by A. E. Van Vogt	76500 — 60¢
OUT OF THE MOUTH OF THE DRAGON by Mark S. Geston	64460 — 60¢
DUNE by Frank Herbert	17260 — 95¢
MEN ON THE MOON Edited by Donald A. Wollheim	52470 — 60¢
THE WARLOCK IN SPITE OF HIMSELF by Christopher Stasheff	87300 — 75¢
THE YELLOW FRACTION by Rex Gordon	94350 — 60¢
THE MERCY MEN by Alan E. Nourse	52560 — 60¢
THE REBEL OF RHADA by Robert Cham Gilman	71065 — 60¢

Available from Ace Books (Dept. MM), 1120 Avenue of the Americas, New York, N.Y. 10036. Send price of book, plus 10¢ handling fee.

JACK VANCE'S
GREAT NEW STRANGE-WORLD SERIES:

PLANET OF ADVENTURE

66899 — 50¢

CITY OF THE CHASCH

Adam Reith is marooned on a world of mysterious aliens and unpredictable dangers.

66900 — 50¢

SERVANTS OF THE WANKH

Quest across the planet Tschai—for freedom, or death?

66901 — 60¢

THE DIRDIR

His route to the stars cut across the planet's deadliest hunting grounds!

66902 — 60¢

THE PNUME

The mystery-shrouded aliens of Tschai held him captive in a labyrinth of terror.

Ask your newsdealer, or order directly from Ace Books (Dept. MM), 1120 Avenue of the Americas, New York, N.Y. 10036. Send price indicated, plus 10¢ handling fee per copy.

ACE DOUBLE BOOKS . . . more for your money

23140 — 60¢
FEAR THAT MAN by Dean R. Koontz
TOYMAN by E. C. Tubb

77710 — 75¢
THE SPACE BARBARIANS by Mack Reynolds
THE EYES OF BOLSK by Robert Lory

81680 — 75¢
TONIGHT WE STEAL THE STARS by John Jakes
THE WAGERED WORLD by L. Janifer & S. J. Treibich

12140 — 75¢
CRADLE OF THE SUN by Brian Stableford
THE WIZARDS OF SENCHURIA by Kenneth Bulmer

42800 — 75¢
KALIN by E. C. Tubb
THE BANE OF KANTHOS by Alex Dain

23775 — 75¢
TREASURE OF TAU CETI by John Rackham
FINAL WAR by K. M. O'Donnell

42900 — 75¢
KAR KABALLA by George H. Smith
TOWER OF THE MEDUSA by Lin Carter

66160 — 75¢
PHOENIX SHIP by W. & L. Richmond
EARTHRIM by Nick Kamin

89250 — 75¢
THE WINDS OF DARKOVER by Marion Z. Bradley
THE ANYTHING TREE by John Rackham

Available from Ace Books (Dept. MM), 1120 Avenue of
the Americas, New York, N.Y. 10036. Send price of book,
plus 10¢ handling fee.